James Urquhart

Mary

And other poems

James Urquhart

Mary
And other poems

ISBN/EAN: 9783744722254

Printed in Europe, USA, Canada, Australia, Japan

Cover: Foto ©Andreas Hilbeck / pixelio.de

More available books at **www.hansebooks.com**

AND OTHER POEMS.

BY

JAMES URQUHART.

—————

DUNDEE:

PRINTED BY JOHN LENG & CO., BANK STREET.

——

1883.

To my Dear Mother.

—)•◦•◦•(—

No mighty name,

In letters large, appears upon this page,

Of Lord or Laird of powerful patronage,

To aid my fame :

No fulsome Ode am I obliged to write,

To feed the vanity of some witless wight,

And lower myself in his and others' sight,

All for a selfish end :

Though all be shrouded in Oblivion's night,

I'll on myself depend.

And, as each line was writ

Because I found a pleasure penning it,

I'll still let Love

Be high above

Each baser passion, when I cast my all

On Literature's rough sea,

Having no hopes to wreck with it, and fall

And overwhelm me.

Therefore I choose

To cull these first-fruits of my doubtful muse

(Convinced that *thou* wilt not the gift refuse),

And offer them to *thee*.

CONTENTS.

———◆◆◆——

MARY:

A SKETCH IN FOUR PARTS.

SPRING.

'Twas morning of a day in Spring's third month—
That time when Earth has just been born again
From out the womb of Winter's chaos dark,
Into Creation's life and light restored;
When Nature, gentle parent, freed from all
The troubles consequent upon her trial,
Has just begun to wipe her weary eyes,
And smile once more serenely through her tears,
And when, revived, she speedily begins
To clothe her offspring in the tender garb
Befitting childhood, woven by herself,
And rich with every difference of shade;
Bedecked with ornaments which can alone

B

Be found within her everlasting stores :—
A garb of emerald verdure, richer far
Than all the gaudy robes of eastern state,
Jewelled with the snowdrop, type of purity,
And heaven-sent token of sweet Innocence ;
And beauteous primrose in the mossy shade,
With every artless grace of modesty ;
And lowly violets, content to dwell
Half hidden 'mong the more ambitious herbs ;
And near to them, the loved forget-me-not,
Drooping its head, and seeming silently
To share the grief of those who once did make
Its fragile flower the type of changeless love
Or lasting friendship, and who since have found
How sadly true the simile has proved,
And what a satire on inconstant man
Hideth beneath the beauty of its name ;
And many a budding tree and curly leaf
Send a fresh thrilling fragrance over all,
And serve as annual heralds of a birth,
Celestial and eternal, that awaits
Our longing souls beyond the dreary tomb
Of this mortality, gladdening our hearts
With the assurance that as Winter seemed

Like as its dreariness would last for aye,
When Springtime suddenly dispelled the gloom,
And cast abroad a universal joy,
So, in due course, will life's dark night away,
And yield its place to never-ending day !
'Twas morning, and the newly-risen sun
Was mounting slowly up the heavenly height,
And shedding from his radiant face of smiles
Beauty and brightness, heat and happiness,
Gliding among the snow-white woolly clouds
That tell of intervening showers to come,
Dispelling from the hills their midnight garb,
And waking earth to life, and joy, and woe.
The dews, like tear-drops in an infant's eyes
(Which, disappearing with the short-lived grief, ·
Add lustre to the beauty of the smile),
Sparkle like diamonds set in finest gold;
And scented odours fresh from opening buds
Are borne upon the exhilarating air.
The woods resound with melodies of birds,
Singing the praises of the early year ;
And streamlets, loosened from their icy bonds,
Sparkling with glee, dance to the merry tunes.
Brightly the morning creeps across the hills

That guard the village, nestling in their shade,
Summoning the labourer to his wonted work,
And sending Hope refreshed into the world:
For Hope is nearest in the early morn,
And loves to dwell among its short-lived hours,
And sport with hearts from which she flies away
As noon comes on, and night succeeds the day.
Nowhere upon the Earth's expansive breadth
Did Springtime lend a lovelier morning-time
Than o'er this village, giving forth a fresh
And brighter beauty to each lowly cot,
Whose only ornament was homeliness;
Dispensing brightness in the sun's young rays,
And freshness from the budding foliage.

'Twas on this morn, and in this village, then,
That Jacob Morris, leaving for his work,
Was standing at his little cottage gate,
Wishing his wife good morning with a kiss;
And waiting near him was a fair young maid,
Who scarce had merged from childhood's tender years,
With fragile form, and timid liquid eyes
Of deep dark blue, and golden, flaxen hair,
That shone and sparkled in the morning sun,

Like waving waters of a sunlit stream ;
Whose modest air bespoke a tender heart,
And in whose gait sweet innocence reposed.

With heart as light as Fancy in a freak,
Forth to his daily work he wends his way,
While Mary sports and gambols by his side,
And cheers him for the labours of the day.

And as they hied along the woods and lanes,
The child would gather wild flowers from the fields,
And gaily decorate her rustic dress,
With all their beauty and variety—
With many a budding rose and daisy pale,
That strove in vain to rival in their hue
The healthy fairness of her loveliness,
And came off losers by comparison.
Now she would hang upon her father's arm,
And sing some little song, in which he'd join
His lusty tones, and chorus as they went ;
When, chancing some gay butterfly to spy,
Away she'd go, careering on in joy,
Chasing the insect on from flower to flower,
And laughing in her aimless playfulness.

While all the time her father smilingly
Would watch her with the anxious eye of love,
And laugh with her, then call her to his side
To vent his feelings in a fervent kiss,
Which she would pay with manifold return,
And walk with him a little hand-in-hand,
And talk of everything she chanced to think of ;
Asking strange questions, which the wisest man
Would fail to answer, but which seemed to her
Quite simple, in her blissful ignorance.

So on they went, while childish innocence
(Itself the soul of all *true* happiness)
Shone like the morning sun in cheering rays,
Upon the heart o'ershadowed with the cares
Of life's experience, till, having walked
Along with him as far as was her wont,
And having placed some wild-flowers in his coat,.
She sweetly turned her pretty mouth to his,
And, with his blessing, hied her home again.
But every now and then she stopped and turned,.
And waited till her father did the same,
Then threw him showers of kisses, that did seem
To make the air far fresher, and the scene

Far brighter, for the beauty of their purity.
And when at last she lost him to her eye,
She went about with childish business
To pick some flowers wherewith to deck the house,
And carry fragrance with her into home.
Gathering the buds in rich profusion strewn
Along the roadside, wandering happily,
She hied along, passing the villagers
Wending their way in batches to their work,
Who often stopped and turned to re-admire
The lovely child, and watch her disappear;
And whose kind looks she'd pay back with a smile,
So pure and modest in its gracefulness,
That even the Angels guarding her young life
Could hardly have surpassed it—till she came
Into the village, and arrived at home.

Oh! what an influence one loved little child
Can have upon the actions of a man,
To keep his wayward footsteps on the path,
And urge him on to new and higher aims!
When wife and friends have failed to wean him from
Some habit long and frequently indulged,
How often does the powerless little babe

Bestir his sluggish conscience and renew him !
'Twas this same influence that, some years ago,
Had weaned poor Jacob from the ways of vice,
And changed a votary of drunkenness
Into a type of honest labourer ;
'Twas such that gave him relish for his work,
And quenched the thirst for sinful licenses,
That armed him strong against Temptation's power,
And made him scorn its base and wily voice.

Mary at home helps mother with her work,
Lending her all her small but willing aid,
Brightening the place, and making labour seem
A pleasant duty to those all around ;
Talking and laughing on incessantly,
And shedding forth o'er all a cheerfulness
That lifts the burden of the hours away,
And causes them to pass so swiftly by
That no one marks the progress of their flight.

Thus merrily they pass the hours of work,
Smoothing the ruggedness of duty's task
With many a work of love, and never feel
The weariness of labour done unwillingly.

Then, having their domestic duties done,
And made the humble little cottage seem
A fairy bower, the mother and her child
Stroll out together 'mong the woods and lanes,
To welcome father coming home from work.
With tidy dress, and singing some old air—
The mother knitting, while the child looks on,
Trying to imitate—they are indeed
A picture of perfected homeliness.

And as they go the evening shadows fall
Slowly, and lengthen 'midst the sun's last rays,
Casting a solemn quietude o'er the scene,
And shading Nature's features for her sleep.
The ploughman looses from his lonely toil,
And takes his dumb companions home to rest;
The shepherd, whistling on his trusty dog,
Assembles all his charges in the fold;
The labourers wend their way to home again,
And rest is regnant o'er the peaceful scene.

Where in the wealthy man's luxurious ease,
That ever breedeth crowds of after ills,
Or in that state of listless indolence

Whose sole reward is ofttimes discontent,
Or where on Earth's wide circle do we find
A pleasure and contentment half so sweet
As that which follows the laborious day,
When, wearied with the toil of honest work,
The honest man enjoys his merited repose?

They meet their father near the village green,
Where at the fall of even the village youth
Met to beguile the evening hours away
In manly sports and innocent delights;
While old folks, mindful of the days gone by,
When their old limbs, now feeble, frail, and stiff,
Could leap and dance with any on the green,
Would sadly grieve to think how soon all there
Must fade and wither like unto themselves,
And leave their sports with others, far behind;
But yet they'd feel a love to linger there,
Where visions of the happiest hours of day
Would flit across their memories' broken glass,
And make them feel in spirit young again,
When aims were high, and every cloud was lined
With the bright edging of a silvery hope,
Dispelling for a time the frozen thoughts—

Those shadows of the grave—that chill the hearts
Of palsied age, thrilling the feeble pulse,
And momentarily giving life renewed.
And then the happy trio hie them home,
Content with life, and having little else.

No anxious thoughts disturb their tranquil rest
Of what to-morrow's ventures may bring in ;
No dreams of riches lost and fortunes won
Molest the mind which poverty becalms :
For peaceful slumber is the sure reward
Of honesty and labour, and befriends
The poor man on his mattress made of straw
Oft'ner than lordlings in their luxury.

In such a quiet and commonplace routine
This happy household went from day to day,
Working for love, and resting but to work,
And all to gain the other's happiness.

And then comes Sunday, God-begotten rest!
Our earthly type of Paradise to come !
Without whose blessed heaven-like repose
This world would waste, and, with'ring, quickly die

It is a gift some sadly underrate,
And oft such take advantage of its peace
To prosecute their longings after ease ;
While others' grumble at its tediousness,
And deem it but a bar to occupation.
The blessed Sabbath, on which God Himself
Did choose to rest in His almighty work,
Is given divinely, and shall mortals dare
To doubt and question its utility ?
When its repose doth follow honest work,
And furnish rest from labour, then it seems
Like kindly showers that freshen parchèd land
And turn it fit for culture, or the blood
Injected into dying man's dried veins,
Which giveth life again, and sends him forth
Unto his work a new and grateful being.
On Sunday Jacob and his loving wife,
With their fair child, dressed in their sober best,
As certain as the parish priest himself,
Went to the little ivied village church,
And heard the Gospel simply preached, and prayed
With thankful hearts and peaceful consciences.

The Minister, a godly good old man,

Told them of Jesus' love, and rich rewards
That are in store, and never raged and raved
About Damnation, Devils, and the Hell
Of everlasting torment, like those fiends,
Calling themselves religious, who believe
That they are safe, and consequently damn
All other creeds more gentle than their own.

And after service of a modest length,
They sometimes met their Pastor in the porch,
And sat with him, or walked among the tombs
Of parted friends, and heard his counsel.   Then,
With his blessing, turned away, and walked
Back to their cottage, talking as they went
To passing friends, and of the things they'd heard.

And if perchance the day proved to be fine,
Their dinner o'er, and having doffed their best,
And donned some homelier vestments, they would go
Admiring God in Nature, some quiet walk
Into the woods ; and, seeking a retreat,
Some shady place, where solemn stillness reigned
O'er all surrounding beauty, there would sit
And listen to the words which Jacob read

From out the Holy Book ; and, having had
Their fill of explanation rudely given
By him to whom all was a mystery,
Would wander on, singing some holy song,
And waking up the echoes of the wood
To praise the Everlasting Deity.
Then home again to have a frugal meal,
At which some next-door friend might chance to be,
To pass the time until the church bell's toll
Summoned them to the house of God again.

The bell rings out, the villagers drop in,
And take their seats with decent reverence ;
And now comes youth, all fresh and cheerily,
With light elastic step, and gaily dressed,
And now old age, drooping its hoary head,
Leaning on staves, with frail and tottering limbs,
Seeming as if this call would be the last.
And Jacob and his wife would early come,
Amidst th' admiring glances of their friends,
While Mary took her seat among the choir,
And sang in hymns the praise of God, while all
Admired her voice, and whispered that she seemed
Like to an angel at the throne above.

'Tis such a life as this I long to lead!
Far from the envious strife and noisy din
Of busy towns, where disappointment feeds
On the torn hearts of many a hopeful youth;
Where Melancholy broods o'er lonely lives
Of learned students, and assists the speed
Of dreary Death, where misery bestrides
The daily street; where vain and pompous pride
Treads down the lowly, and bedecks itself
With every outward ornament of worth;
Where vice is rampant and conspicuous,
When holiness and goodness should prevail;
And prostitution, rotting in the streets,
Contaminates the fairest of our race.
Oh! how I sigh for rural solitude,
Where every thought darts freely thro' the mind,
Where peace presides o'er all, and where the soul
Of man may rest, if such it can on Earth!
There, hushed to sleep by streamlets' melody,
And wakened by the hymns of heavenly larks,
Roaming thro' woods, enraptured with the lays
Of beauteous birds, and worshipping my God
In Nature's Temple, let me live a life
Of innocent content, and happy die!

SUMMER.

Summer hath cast her mantle o'er the scene,
And clothed the meadows in a richer green,
Hath given new colour to the rip'ning corn,
And fragrant freshness to the dewy morn.
The heather blooms upon the mountain tops,
And wild flowers mingle with the verdant crops,
The dewdrops nestle in the perfumed flowers,
And sunbeams dance among the morning showers.
The nightingale singing out his heartfelt love,
The hymns of larks heard softly from above,
The blackbird whistling on a lowly tree,
The rippling streamlet with its melody,
The ringing woods, the verdure of the trees,
The universal harmony of busy bees—
All are the heralds of the joyous mirth
Which Summer scatters freely o'er the Earth.

Summer—when every beauty decks the vale,
And every songster swells the tuneful gale,
When from their clover beds the larks arise
To sing their hymns among the morning skies,

When clouds but come to quickly pass away,
And lend a varied beauty to the day,
Summer hath come, all Nature tells the tale,
From loftiest summit down to deepest vale !

Now Nature, like a lovely rosy maid,
In all the charms of healthfulness arrayed,
Just ere she enters on her womanhood,
Smiling on all, and with a multitude
Of ways engaging, bright and ofttimes coy,
Lends unto all her own apparent joy.

The woods, with every leaf of foliage crowned,
With ivied trunks, and wild flowers strewn around,
Where, hanging from the intertwining trees,
The honeysuckle scents the cooler breeze,
Are filled with warblings and the mild perfume
Of budding wild flowers bursting into bloom.
There 'mong the mossy knolls and ferny dells
Romance and Poetry enweave their spells
About the worldly traveller's heated brain,
And bid him taste of Paradise again.
The bubbling stream, melodious as it flows
Through shady glens, or where it dancing goes

c

'Midst golden sunbeams, tinkling like a bell,
Mingles its music in the joyful swell.   .

How sweet it is, how ravishingly sweet,
After a toil beneath the summer's heat
To lay one down in some old shady wood,
To rest awhile and dream in solitude!
How the glad song-birds trill on every tree!
How musical the streamlets seem to be!
How fresh and verdant from without, where all
Labour beneath the Sun's enslaving thrall!
Here, by the brink of some clear crystal pool,
The air is fresh, the zephyr's breath is cool,
And over all the shaded loveliness
Dwells a deep sense of liberty and peace;
And, listless laid where everything is still,
Our wayward thoughts would wander at their will,
Or, cradled by Nature to repose, we find
A balm to soothe the troubles of the mind.

Of all the seasons that bedeck the scene
With varied splendours, Summer reigns the queen;
For every charm which Springtime's freshness lent
Is now matured and lovelier " cent. per cent."

No sudden clouds now dim the sun's clear ray,
And sullen mar the beauty of the day;
But from the early morn till twilight's fall,
An azure sky spreads brightly over all.
And when the Sun in glorious state has set,
Its crimson light, departing, lingers yet,
As if 'twere loth to go, then slowly dies,
And from the East the night's dark shadows rise.

This is the time when Beauty from her throne
In heaven descends, and claims the Earth her own;
When to her shrine from Industry and Arts
Poor mortals come to sacrifice their hearts—
The farmer, wearied with his Springtime's toil,
Now rests him from his labours for a while,
And, having done his duty, leaves to God
To rear the harvests from the seeds he's sowed.
The pale-faced Clerk now shuts his musty books,
And hies him off to sport beside the brooks;
Or, tourist clad, as Highland mountaineer,
Fatigues himself where sportsmen chase the deer;
The learned Judge doffs the judicial wig,
(That shallow hoax to make the man look big),
And Justice chaste, on doubtful pleasures bent,

Sets out to " do" the *well*-known Continent ;
The ragged urchin now can happy be,
And for a time forget his misery ;
And pedagogues shut up the ponderous tome,
And send their prisoners to the longed-for home.

'Tis in Life's summer when our hopes are strong,
Ere yet we've mingled in the world's vast throng
Of striving, cheating, suffering, and woe,
That any of Earth's few fleet sweets we know ;
Ere forth into Life's battle we have rushed,
Before youth's darling fancies have been crushed ;
When every star that shines upon us seems
To point realisation of our dreams.

Now to our tale.   Some years have glided by
Since last we left our little family,
But every day and every year has been
Passed in the simple, loving old routine ;
Except that, in the closing of last year,
Poor Jacob lost his life-companion dear,
And Mary a fond mother.   Oh ! how hard it seemed,
Just when the sun of happiness had beamed
Upon their household, that Death's sombre cloud

Should gather round and all Life's pleasures shroud.

But as the calm that follows tempests o'er

Seems far more tranquil than it was before,

So this small household, quite resigned at last,

Could think regretless on the happy past ;

And oftentimes, when twilight bathed the scene,

And evening falling shadowed all serene,

Returning from the labours of the day,

They'd cross the churchyard on their homeward way,

And rest them where the lost loved one was laid

To sleep beneath the church tower's sheltering shade.

The lovely child, so gentle and so good,

Has now attained her early womanhood,

Replete with every charm and every grace,

And stands confessed the beauty of the place ;

No empty pride, no well perfected art,

Soils the pure utterings of her simple heart,

But, innocent herself, she fears no ill,

And every action follows on her will ;

Guided by Nature in simplicity,

Her words and life are clothed with purity ;

Nor rigid forms nor icy etiquette

About her manner their cold shades beget.

How unlike that fair beauty of the world—
Powdered and painted, pampered up, and curled,
Till every feature of her first creation
Is either lost or hid in affectation !

'Twas evening now, and everything was still,
Save for the murmuring of some distant rill,
Or nightingale's sweet vesper ; twilight's shade,
Brooded serenely over hill and glade ;
The rising Moon just sent the faintest beam
Thro' the dark trees above upon the stream,
Spreading a fairy lustre where it fell,
And deepening the darkness of the dell.

There in the peaceful solitude and shade
Of arching foliage, the same fair maid,
Pensive and sad, beside the streamlet lay,
Watching its wavelets as they fled away ;
And as she watched the waters disappear,
Now sparkling bright, now darksome-like and drear,
She thought of her past life, how bright it was,
And how it now seemed dark and dull, because
She loved in doubt—but, whether dark or bright,
The waters hurried on and vanished out of sight.

She murmured low, " How happy would I be
If I but knew he really lovèd me!
Fain would I quell the doubts that will impart
The pangs of sorrow to my doting heart;
In vain I strive to calm my rising fears,
And stem the torrent of those wilful tears.
Yet, why should I repine?   Hath he not said,
That I, so lowly, am the only maid
His heart hath ever owned?   Can I not trust
The word I love so well?   Yet fears will thrust
Their dreary shades upon the darkening sky
Of my soul's happiness.   'Tis strange that I
Should love and basely doubt!   Nor can I tell
Of any reason that this dreary spell
Should cast a dimness over every light,
And shed at noon the sadness of the night;
Yet all may be but fancies of a brain,
Where only Love's contending thoughts remain!
Oh! that yon orb, whose silv'ry rays illume
This fairy stream, could chase the dismal gloom
That's settled on my soul, and cause the ray
Of trustful love to light my heart alway!"

Thus wrapt in thought, she sees not draw her near

The object, loved, of all her hopes and fear,
Until he, treading on the underwood,
With crackling noise, disturbs the solitude ;
She starts, and views him with an eager gaze.
Half frightened and surprised, and then repays
The kiss of his fair greeting.   Oh ! can words relate
The thrilling joy she felt, the heavenly state
Her soul delighted knew ?   Her doubts and fears,
Like morning mists, whene'er the sun appears,
Vanished and fled, nor left a trace behind,
To soil the bliss that brightened up her mind.
How eagerly his every word she hears—
The lying term that flatters and endears,
The promise never kept !   How every kiss
Is treasured by her soul !   Her happiness
Is now wrapt up in him.   Oh ! can it be
That such a love will reap but misery ?

But now they walk, and as they wend their way
Without the den, the full resplendent ray
Of night's fair guardian floods the dewy scene,
And bathes the woodlands in a silv'ry sheen.
And each, with different feelings of delight,
View the soft splendours of the Summer's night,

When the hot sun, with all its gaudy glare,
Has run its course, and left the heated air
To cool among the moonlight, and when every dale
Is wrapt in solemn shadow, and the gale
Is hardly heard, as, perfumed with the best
Of Nature's sweets, it murmurs from the west.
'Tis now, when night has chased the busy day,
With all its fleeting fortunes far away,
And caused its strife and noisy din to cease,
That Nature rests, and from the realms of peace
A heavenly calm succeedeth, and 'tis now
The mind reposes, and the fevered brow
Is cooled in needful sleep.
    Still on they go,
Chatting of things that only lovers know,
And only lovers interest, until they come,
With slow, unwilling footsteps nearer home.

Waiting to say the long put-off " Good-night,"
They linger 'midst the pale and pure moonlight,
Beside the churchyard wall, whilst Mary shows—
" Just where that lonely weeping willow grows,"
Her mother's resting-place—a little mound
Of well-trimmed grass, with branches neatly bound.

And for a time a silence fell o'er all,
And both were lost in thought.   Did not the call
Of conscience ring throughout his heart, and make
Remorse o'ercome design ?   Did he not quake
To face the strength of innocence ?   Ah ! when
The fire of carnal love is lit in men,
Not all the forces of their minds can stay
The horrid power from wielding full its sway !

Truly she looked most fair as there she stood,
With one soft hand in his, her charms imbued
With welling love and gratitude ; her eyes,
Of ocean's depth, and blue as Naples' skies,
With wistful looks were gazing on the place
Where her lost guide lay sleeping ; o'er her face
Passed just a tinge of sadness, while he told
His tale of love—" What tho' the flowers unfold
Their varied forms and sweeten every lea
With od'rous breathings; tho' on every tree
The nightingale pours forth his am'rous note,
And on the zephyrs music makes to float—
If thou art absent from me !   Let the skies
Hang cloudless as they will, my dazzled eyes
Will show them dull and dreary, if may be

They wander from thy brightness!   All to me,
When thou art gone, is like a summer's day
When mists have chased all cheerfulness away.
Life would without thee be but lengthened pain,
Too frightful even in fancy to sustain ;
More dread than death itself in all its drear
And dismal mystery, for hope and fear,
And their attendant miseries, all sink
Into the Grave's oblivion.   Oh ! but think
On Springtime robbed of every tender flower,
Of clouded Summer days that ever lower,
On Heaven without the light of God, and see
My life on earth, my love, devoid of thee !"

"Hush ! Hush ! enough ! for I now swear to you
By all I hold most sacred, I shall bear you true.
To-night has given a happiness to me,
Which I once sadly thought could never be,
Yet prayed for daily.   Many a heavy hour
I've watched, regardless of sleep's potent power,
And kept love's weary vigils, while my breast,
Tossed with an ever present wild unrest,
Bore its grim load alone, nor dared to ope
Its smallest corner to a ray of hope

Which seemed to shine in mockery, and give
But better light wherein Despair might live.
Thus had I gone all lonely on my way,
Sorrowing in secret, on from day to day,
Till the long sighed-for light of heaven at last
Had chased away the sorrows of the past.
But now that all these dismal fears are fled,
And once again the balm of peace is shed
Upon my gladdened soul, henceforth I strive
To prove me worthy of thee, and contrive
To show my love by my devotedness,
And making thy will mine, and only peace
And love will be our portion."

　　　　　　　　Listening intent,
Folding her in his arms, he downward bent,
And kissed the earnest face, now glad, and free
From doubt, yet full of lovely modesty.

After a lingering kiss, and having said
The necessary " Good-night," so long delayed,
They hie them to their homes.　But not until
The dark'ning night and intervening hill
Baffled her sight did Mary think to stay

Her honeyed showers of kisses, and obey
Her struggling sense of duty.
                    When alone,
And left with nothing stirring but his own
Unrestful conscience and the mournful wind,
Conflicting sentiments disturbed his mind,
And rendered him unhappy.·

            ·   " Would this tie
Were loosened and undone ! I wonder why
My resolutions are of no avail
To carry out my purposes, and fail
Even before they're tried. I did not count
On this result, on such a foul amount
Of sick'ning love rot. Yet I cannot suit
My actions to my will, nor yet refute
That tyrant will, for it has gone too far
To stomach disappointment. Can I mar
So much of innocence, and break a heart
That obviously is mine, whose every part
Is strong in trustfulness in me ? Oh, God !
It must not, cannot be ! Yet still the road
Backwards from vice is harder far to trace
Than that to greater sin, for every pace

Is fraught with memories of deeds which rise
Afresh in our repentance.   All my daring dies,
Killed by her innocence, and in its fall
Shatters my fondest wishes, plans and all;
Henceforth I shall avoid her, and endeavour
To banish from my mind her form for ever.
This seems to be the only open course
To rescue her, and save me from remorse,
The sting of which would kill.   For well I know
Her sight would set my passions all aglow,
And overcome my reason.   Yet in this
I break my vow, and scatter all the bliss
My lies created.   No! whate'er betide,
I must appear devoted, and abide
My opportunity.   I hear the voice
Of conscience still amid the clanging noise
Of all my passions.   And methinks I feel
An unknown strangeness o'er my senses steal,
Wak'ning my soul to pity.   Can it be
That I have fallen into Love's snare, and she
Unwitting is the fowler?   But my mind
Refuses counsel, and I cannot find
A path in this inextricable maze
To lead me out again, for all the ways

Run foul of one another, and return
To their detested source.   How I do mourn
That e'er I took one step into a place
I cannot keep, or quit without disgrace !"

Musing thus on he went, while up on high
The Moon withdrew her light, and o'er the sky
Night reigned supremely darksome—all around,
Save his own soul, was wrapt in peace profound.

As when the sea o'er which some direful blast,
Driving the crested waves, has newly past,
Rests in unbroken calm, so Mary's mind
Reposed, 'mid sweet tranquillity reclined.
And slumbering on in love, dreaming of naught
But coming days with Hope's fair fancies fraught ;
Thus peacefully she passed her time away,
Cheerful and happy, while from day to day
Her faith was fed with promises renewed,
And faith made bright the future which imbued
The present with sweet hopes.

                    Jacob, the while,
Works on as usual at his daily toil

Willingly, and all for Mary—all that she
May never know the pangs of poverty.
But hard enough it is, for tho' the day
Be passed from morn till eve in work, the pay
Of sweat is insignificant, compared
With all the hoards which Indolence hath shared.
Yet, uncomplaining, working aye the same,
Day after day he furthers on his aim.

Like to the stag, reclining where the fen
Seems thick and safe, and far from mortal ken,
That, happy in the deemed security,
Rests his proud antlered head, bethinking he
Is safely hid, while even then the eyes
Of some keen ghillie, peering where he lies,
Select him for the chase, this happy home
Lived all unconscious of the grief to come.

AUTUMN.

The year is wearing on. The withered leaves
Fall gently from the baring trees o'erhead,
With rustling melody, and on the ground,
In waste profusion, with'ring fast away,
Lie Summer's loveliest ornaments. Upon the hills
The corn no longer waves in rippling gold ·
Beneath a burnished sun; the reapers' song;
No longer floats along the harvest field,
And stimulates the labourer; the dreary woods
Invite no more the traveller from his way;
For now the nightingale has ceased to weave
His daily music, and the shrill east winds
Now pipe discordantly where gentle zephyrs
Were wont to breathe their harmony. And now
The sickly sun, tired with the cheerless prospect,
Seeks earlier towards the west, denying us
The heavenly twilight, and its hallowed peace;
And envious Night, from out her eastern caves,
When the red sun has sunk in hasty state,
Claims Earth her own, nor waits that decent time
For Day's interment. Over Nature's face

D

There rests a tinge of sadness, that reflects
Its shadow on the onlooker, and thrills
The soul with thoughtfulness.   The chilly winds
Sweep o'er the dismal plain in fitful gusts,
And whistle 'mong the woodlands, heralding
The keener blasts of Winter, fast approaching.
Adown the dell the dreary scene extends,
For the damp path is strewn with rotting leaves
And dying wild flowers, and the trees above
Are dark and shivering dismally ; the stream,
Dirty with mud, and swollen by the rains,
Has lost its silver melody, and whirls
Its eddying waters onward.   All the birds,
No longer seeking shelter from the sun,
Have left the shade, and silence and decay
Rest there together.   Over all the scene
Autumn is growing old, and wearing done !

The village, sheltered by the neighbouring hill
From the bleak blast, lies snugly in the vale,
And proves itself a welcome resting-place
For the tired peasant trudging home from work
When evening falls in drear and chilling shadows
Over the wind-swept plain, inviting him

To cheery hearths and family repose—
His almost sole reward.   The village green
Is nearly now forsaken, and the dance
And outdoor fun are over, while the inn,
A homely hearty house, is patronised
Night after night by cheerful companies
Of merry-hearted fellows, who, with tales
Of dread and mirth, beguile the lonely time .
In harmless occupation.   Cynics sneer,
And talk of this as wrong ; but let such live
An isolated peasant life, and learn
Whether they would not spend a few odd pence
To purchase company.   The village wives
Are seen no longer at the even's fall,
Knitting their homely work or gossiping
Beside their cottage doors, but, social too,
Betake them to some neighbour's gathering
To drink the fragrant cup, and have their fill
Of news and scandal, which no mortal woman
I ever met with really disliked.

One year has winged its flight into the past
And dropped into eternity, since last we left
Jacob and Mary in their happiness,

All unmolested.   Since then things have changed,
And sadly so.   The sun of joy hath set,
And night is coming on ; the horizon
Is banking up with storm-clouds thick and black,
Darkening the sky, and warning that ere long
The angry storm will rage with fiercesome fury !
But Mary still believes, in innocence,
That there is hope, and trusts the promises
Made to ensnare her ; and thus, strong in faith,
She bears her weary secret hopefully.
Poor gentle Mary, what a sorrow thine !
How thy poor, wounded, trustful heart must ache
Beneath so great a burden !   Oh ! so young,
So good, so innocent, to be destroyed !

The evening shades are darkening into night,
And chill the night-wind whirls around the cot
Where live our little family.   Within
A cheerful fire is burning in the grate,
And lighting up the room.   A frugal meal
Is spread upon a table neat and clean,
In homely luxury   Upon the hearth
A pair of shoes are basking in the blaze,
Cosy and warm, and in a corner snug

From every draught, the arm-chair has been placed
Ready for Jacob.
        Mary flits about,
Anxious to add more comfort all around,
Now listening to some footstep passing by
To recognise her Father's, now engaged
In some small loving labour.   Yet the while
Her busy hands are tending to their work,
A deep sad sigh would augur that her thoughts
Were wand'ring wearily, and far away
From present happiness.   And now she sits
Down by the fire to wait till Jacob's step
Shall sound upon the threshold, and reward
Her loving preparations for his coming.
The lamp is still unlit, and on the walls
And floor and roof fantastic shadows dance
Among the quivering firelight, and beget
Strange, fanciful designs.   In reverie deep,
Mary thinks on, now gazing in the fire
With wistful look, now watching eagerly
The changing shadows.   On that pensive face
Sadness is regnant where, not long ago,
Beamed perfect happiness.   The tender roses
Have vanished from her cheeks, and lilies pale

Usurp their places now.   The deep blue eyes,
That once were wont to sparkle with delight
And overflow with gladness, now express
In their sad loveliness the gnawing grief
That dwells within her soul.   Oh, what a change !
The budding freshness of the Spring has gone !
The Summer's flowers have faded in decay !
And Autumn's winds are chilling now !   How soon
The wintry blasts will howl and devastate !

Jacob arrives, and, wakened from her thoughts,
Mary starts up to greet him, and receive
The usual salutation of a kiss.
And now the lamp is lit, and cheerily
The rosy fire burns up, no longer fraught
With weird fantastic shades, and laughingly
Leaps up the cheerful chimney ; and the ghosts
That revelled in the firelight disappear,
And all is bright again.
         Though tired and hungry,
His meal is not partaken of before
He renders humble thanks for it and all
The comforts of his life.   Thus he enjoys
It all the better for his having done

His easy duty first.   A welcome meal,
And honestly discussed ! for labour lends
A keener edge unto the appetite
Than any artificial stimulant.
Hence the poor labourer with his musty crust,
His hunk of cheese and pot of home-brewed ale,
Is satisfied, while epicures with tastes
Unnatural, and self-created, wade
'Mong rarities heaped up, in vain to find
A dish to please their palates.

Being done,
And all things cleared away and rendered neat
By Mary's carefulness, old Jacob sits
In the accustomed arm-chair, resting him
After his day's fatigue.   How lovingly
He talks to her of all the day's events,
And of to-morrow's projects, while she hears,
And listens sadly silent !   Now and then
Her glances, brightening at some word of love,
Would rest upon his face, and then withdrawn,
Become again enshadowed.   Till at length
He bids her to come nearer, so that he
May fondle and caress as was his wont

When seated in the evening.   But each touch
Of his dear hand thrills her racked mind with thoughts
Sad and soul-piercing, and she even dares
To think of telling her fond father all,
And plead her innocence.   But, ah ! she knows
That in the knowledge of her misery
His loving heart would break ; so she refrains,
And keeps her weary secret to herself.

Thus, talking of the dear one long since lost,
And happy days gone by, and times to come,
When from the savings of his well-earned means
He should be able to give over toil,
And be nigh Mary always, night wore on.

And now the day's last duty is performed,
For Mary, taking down the Family Bible,
Reads a small portion of the heavenly word,
While Jacob listens eagerly.   For now
His sight is not so good as it has been,
And somehow, too, he loves to hear her read
The Holy Book ; for all her tender nature
Shows in her reverential air, and minds him
Of his first Mary, gone to where she seemed

To have been sent him from.   Then, kneeling down,
Jacob repeats a little prayer, and then
They part them for the night—Jacob to rest
In welcome slumber, Mary to revolve
Her restless thoughts within her harassed mind.

And now when all the world is at peace,
And bathed in slumber, and the feeble light
Is flickering in the draught, while from without
The sighing of the night wind lone is heard
Among the leafless trees, and everything
That lent a passing brightness to her life
Has gone, the dreary shadows creep again
Across her anguished soul, and for a time
Even Hope, life's latest lightener, is obscured.

But the morning came again, and shed its brightness
Over the joyous Earth, and Hope, revived,
Strengthened its fluttering rays within her soul,
And gave her peace.

Thus with each dawning day
New prospects cheered her but to pass away,
And leave her soul still darker than before.

Looking as happy as she can when fears,
Unformed and dark, are cankering in her heart,
And putting on faint smiles which all reflect
Her sorrow in their loveliness, she meets
· Her father early risen from his rest,
And tends with carefulness to all the wants
Of morning time.   The breakfast has been set
In spotless cleanliness, and in his wallet
Some wholesome fare is placed, and everything
Within the little cot is neat and nice,
And fresh as morning's self.

        As was her wont
In past and happier days, when every thought
Was all of joy and wonder, Mary still,
When seasons will permit, accompanies
Her father in the morning to his work.
And great the disappointment of them both,
If Nature, jealous, with untimely shower,
Prevent this little joy.

        So, having breakfasted,
And rendered thanks, they leave their little home
Together, arm in arm, as long ago ;
Only that now the arm that needs support
Is Jacob's, and the gaysome little child

Is there no more to chase the butterfly,
And pluck the rival roses, and the song
No longer wakes the echoes as they go ;
For, with a face still fair and beautiful,
But now by care o'ershadowed, Mary walks
With sad and sobered steps.   Her deep blue eyes
Seem gazing far away upon events
Unseen to all save her.   With many a word
Of anxious love does Jacob try to win
The smile that in the mornings long since past
Brightened the way, back to her face again.

The Autumn morning, bright and brown and chill,
Reigns o'er the prospect, and the early sun,
Newly arisen, and undimmed by day,
Sheds o'er the landscape now his clearest ray.
The road is thickly strewn with fallen leaves
Huddled in batches, thickest at the side,
O'er which, as o'er the moss-grass in the woods,
A crispy rime has fallen, clothing all
In glittering whiteness.   O'er the arching sky
Not one dark cloud careers, but, deep and pure,
It compasseth the landscape.   Summer's breath
Seems for a time to mingle with the winds

Of aged Autumn, and the morning sheds
A transient life into the dying scene.

The pathway passes through the little churchyard,
And leads them by the little grassy mound
Where Mary's mother sleeps—a resting-place
One well might envy.　O'er the well-trimmed grass
Upon the grave a silvery covering
Of hoar-frost pure has fall'n, reminding them,
Not of the dead, but of the spotless robe
Of heavenly immortality that clothes
The ransomed soul, unsullied by the flesh,
Which onward soars to God.　A soothing sight,
And breathing hope and peace.　But Mary, wretched,
Sees also there a type of that pure state
Which now is hers no more, and shame and fear
Gnaw at her poor heart, broken and betrayed.

This morning somehow Mary does not go
So far as usual.　Stopping at the stile,
A mile beyond the churchyard, she receives
The parting kiss, and turns her back again.

The morning now is merging into day,

And banking clouds are gathering in the sky,
Dimming Aurora's brightness ; chill the breeze
Is rising up, and whistling thro' the branches,
Mourning the sun's lost rays ; and suddenly
The day that opened with so bright a morn
Is overcast and dreary.

        Mary sits,
Long after leaving Jacob, near the stile,
Watching the change, and listening to the wind,
And fancying in its dreary lonesome sighing
A sorrow corresponding with her own.
Thus pensive here she stayed, till drops of rain,
Blown chilly on her cheek, awakened her
From out her reverie.   Then wearily,
And with a deep-drawn sigh, she rose and walked
Towards her home.   But scarcely had she risen
And brushed a trembling tear-drop from her eye,
When in the distance, walking hurriedly,
She saw her lover drawing near to her.
Once more a lustre brightens in her eyes !
Again her heart beats quick with eager hope !
A crimson hue is mantling o'er her face,
And her expectant bosom heaves and throbs.

Now sorrow flies away and fears depart,
And only joy is regnant in her heart!
For the long interval of doubt and dread
Since last she saw him has now all gone by,
And happiness returns.   Oh ! what a wild
And thrilling joy is coursing thro' her mind !

Dressed in a hunting suit, which well set off
His shapely figure, he, in face and limb,
Is very handsome, as he takes her hand,
And prints a kiss upon her glowing cheek.
But somehow he averts his face from hers,
When she is telling him how glad she is
To see him once again, and in his eyes
There is a look of shame and sadness hid ;
But soon 'twas gone, and o'er his handsome features
Passed a fixed look of firm determination.

Not long the gladness is unmixed with fear
Within poor Mary's heart.   The fervent tones
Of burning love strike on her ear no more !
The tender looks are gone !   The gentle touch
No more encircles her !   Oh what a change !
Oh what a disappointment to her soul !

And now a silence ensues as they walk
Apart and thoughtful ; while poor Mary's heart
Sinks in the deep dark waters of despair,
And he is struggling hard within himself
For bravery enough to overcome
His conscience, which destroys and enervates
Each resolution formed.
   At last he speaks—
" Mary, when last we met, I gave to you
A promise, that ere many months had gone
You would become my wife ; and still I swear
I now would implement it ; but my will
No longer rules my actions."

   Here he paused,
And nothing broke the silence save the sobs
That burst convulsively from Mary's breast,
Plunged in the direst agony of grief,
As on they walked apart.

   " My love for you
Is as it was at first, and nothing changed,
And never will be otherwise—but still
I dare not keep that promise. Everything

Prevents me !   For my very means of life
Would be denied to me did I refuse
To do my father's pleasure.   But although
You may not be my own, if you should want
The slightest comfort, only let me know,
And I will grant it you."

                  An angry flush
Burned in her face at this, but quickly died,
And all was calm again.   The scalding tears
Fell thick, and dimmed the vision of her eyes,
Till all around seemed like some misty dream,
In which there dwelt no hope.   No angry word
Escaped her quivering lips ; no vile reproach
Was hurled at her deceiver, but one look—
One longing, tearful, broken-hearted look—
Was all.   Yet what a thunderbolt
It seemed to him—piercing his very soul,
Burning remorse into his tortured heart,
And casting him to earth.   Transfixed he stood,
And viewed the wreck of loveliness and worth
His cruel words had made, and for a time
He knew not how to act; while Mary still
Was weeping bitterly her untold sorrow.

Slowly he made towards her, and imprinted
A farewell kiss upon her passive cheek,
And then in silence left her there alone—
Alone and broken-hearted!

   Chill the wind
Blew up again, and fanned her fevered face,
And rain-drops mingled with her hot salt tears,
Unheeded all by her. And now she came,
With half-unconscious step, and weeping still,
Into the little churchyard. There the frost
Had vanished from the grass, and left the grave
Dreary and damp beneath the sombre shadow
Thrown by the Church's tower. Here, hid from all,
She cast her on her mother's resting-place,
And told her sorrow to the silent dead.
Poor, trustful, loving Mary! There she lay,
In all the anguish of a breaking heart,
While high above the wind made melody,
Lonesome and fitful round the watchful tower,
And all around the rain-drops pattered fast.
Long thus she lay, and not until the shadows
Began to darken did she rise and wend
Her weary way towards a hopeless home.

WINTER.

The snow lies deep on the hidden ground,
　And the trees are thin and bare,
The air is cold, and the peace profound
　Of Winter is everywhere.

A leaden hue is o'er all the sky,
　And the frost is hard and keen,
And the sun has hid in a shroud on high,
　As if sick of the dreary scene.

The birds that sang in the leafy shade,
　Are far, far away o'er the seas ;
And the only sound is the moaning made
　By the wind among the trees.

The song of the stream we no longer hear
　Blending with notes o'erhead ;
For the lonely dell is now dismally drear,
　And its waters are frozen dead.

Some snowflakes float in the chilly air,
   Left of the storm just o'er ;
But it does not seem that the calm will last,
   For the sky is threatening sore.

Jacob has left some time ago,
   And Mary is sitting alone,
Gazing through tears on the waste of snow
   And wrapt in thoughts all her own.

For there's no one to whom she may tell her grief,
   And ease her aching heart ;
Nowhere to look to to gain relief
   From her heart-wound's ruthless smart.

So she looks out to-day on the dreariness
   Of a waste of untrodden snows,
While within her heart is the weariness
   Of a grief that no respite knows.

How often she longs for her mother's breast,
   Whereon to lay her head ;
And sighs as she thinks of the peaceful rest
   Among the churchyard's dead !

The face is pale that was once so bright,
  And care sits on that brow;
The deep blue eyes have lost their light
  And are wells of sorrow now.

The thought that burns within her brain,
  Is that Jacob must shortly share
Her deepening shame, and her grief and pain,
  And it drives her to despair.

For she knows full well when her secret is known
  That his heart must surely break;
For all his hope is in her alone,
  And he lives but for her sake.

Oh! what can she do?   To her troubled mind,
  One only course seems right—
To leave her father and home behind,
  And hide all her shame in flight.

Poor Mary! It is but an idle thought,
  Oh! where will you wander to?
For the drifts are deep, and the roads are fraught
  With dangers all new to you!

But the constant thoughts of her shame and care
 Have done their direful part;
And a mind endarkened by black despair
 Is allied to a broken heart.

And she never once thought of the wintry day,
 Or where she would find a place
To rest her at night, but of flying away
 And hiding her deep disgrace.

Oh! the restless throbs of a troubled breast!
 Oh! the pain of a broken heart!
Oh! the grief-stricken mind that knows no rest
 From despair that will not depart!

The bleak wintry wind was rising high,
 And 'twas dark, though not yet late,
As with tearful eye, and a deep-drawn sigh,
 She passed through the wicket gate.

But before she turned to hurry away,
 She stood for a moment and gazed
At the dear little home she was leaving that day,
 And her eyes grew dim and dazed.

What visions wild ran through her brain,
    Confused, and weird, and dread ;
While excitement was coursing thro' every vein
    And heating her aching head !

Trembling with fear and the piercing blast,
    She passed through the village unseen ;
For all were inside, and the doors shut fast—
    The wind was so bitterly keen.

And hurrying on, she left behind
    The village all still and white,
Immerging itself as the day declined
    In the gathering mists of night.

Yet further on, and a little hill
    Raised up its dark brow between
Herself and the home that she looked for still,
    And closed up the dreary scene.

Then her heart sank low in the ebon tide
    Of a dismal and deep despair,
As she looked all around her on every side,
    And saw nothing but bleakness there.

And alas ! what hope has she further on,
    That she hurries so on her way ?
Oh none, oh none, for all hope is gone
    With the one she has left for aye.

As she hurried along now the lowering sky
    Grew darker and darker amain,
And the snowflakes began to go whirling by,
    And crowd in the air again.

And now and then some peasants passed
    Hieing them home for the night;
And many a curious look they cast
    At the strange unusual sight.

For they wondered how Jacob's much-loved child
    Should be out in such terrible weather;
And many a guess and conjecture wild
    They made as they trudged together.

But they went on their way, and soon forgot
    Poor Mary with all her woes;
And each in his turn sought his own little cot,
    And the sweetness of sound repose.

The sky above is one fell black cloud,
   And the flaked snow, swift eddying falls;
And the cold north-wind is shrieking loud
   In fierce and fitful squalls.

Bitter the wind as it blusters by,
   Whirling the falling snow,
Shaking the trees so gaunt and high,
   And chasing the drifts below!

Yet she bravely strives with the Winter's night
   And the drift and the piercing blast;
But the strongest nerve in such a fight
   Must fail in its strength at last.

Her body is thoroughly tired and worn,
   And her footsteps are wearing slow;
While her poor bleeding heart is rent and torn
   By the poisoned wedge of woe.

So, weary in body, and wretched in mind,
   Reckless to live or to die,
With Despair wrapping all, before and behind,
   In a dreadful obscurity:

Staggering with faintness, she seeks the side
   Of the road, and lying down there,
Where the hedge and the tall trees somewhat hide
   Her form from the frosty air :—

She falls to sleep. For a little time
   Her bosom is free from pain,
And in dreamland's mystic shadowy clime .
   She is happy at home again.

Thus she slumbers in peace on that cold, cold bed,
   And her poor pretty face the while,
White as the face of the newly dead,
   Is wreathed in a faint sad smile.

Meantime the blustering storm has passed,
   And hushed is the howling wind,
And a stillness over the scene is cast,
   Like the rest of an anxious mind.

And the calm, cold Moon sheds her quivering light
   O'er the glittering snow-covered lea ;
Till the robes of the changeful wintry night
   Are of beauteous purity.

Suddenly from her snow-covered couch
   Like a startled deer she sprang,
With a wild fixed eye, and a loud weird cry
   On the midnight air there rang.

Then she laughed outright a blood-curdling laugh,
   In a terrible joyless glee ;
And her eyes shone bright with unearthly light—
   She had sunk in insanity !

"How brightly the moonbeams are dancing to-night!
   And how lovely the world seems to be !
Surely heaven's blessed portals must soon be in sight,
   For I've sought long and anxiously !

"Oh, let me be on !   I hear voices behind,
   That would call me from heaven's very gate ;
Sing on, ye bright angels, and lead me to find
   My way, or 'twill soon be too late.

"Oh ! the music I hear ! How it thrills all my heart,
   How it causes my eyes to o'erflow !
How it brightens my mind, and sheds balm on the smart
   That my soul sustained long, long ago !

" My anguish is gone. Yet I shudder to cast
    One thought on the life that is o'er,
Or the terrible valley thro' which I have passed,
    Even when they can frighten no more.

".Yes, Sorrow and Shame, ye have harassed me sore,
    : And traced those deep lines on my brow ;
But, tyrants, your long reign of agony's o'er—
    I am free from your tyranny now !

" Poor father ! 'twas selfish to leave you, I know,
    In a world where there's nothing but sadness ;
But, oh ! had I lingered much longer below,
    'Twould have driven me surely to madness."

Thus she spoke, while the scalding tears coursed down
        her cheek,
    Pale as the Moon's pallid ray ;
And then all in eagerness turned her to seek
    The path of her heavenly way.

Poor Mary ! Oh, God ! can this possibly be
    The fair child that was seen one Spring morning,
Not yet long ago, in the midst of her glee,
    With wild flowers her gay dress adorning ?

What a change! Yet still, one can easily trace
   The features so tender and fair,
And the sweet smile that lit up the heavenly face
   'Mid a glory of golden-waved hair.

How lovely she looks in the Moon's placid beam,
   With her hair spreading loose o'er her breast;
While her deep azure eyes turned to heaven brightly
     gleam
   With a happiness fully expressed!

Oh! the heavenly joy of a sorrow past!
   Oh! the balm for a broken heart!
Oh! the blissful rest which is gained at last,
   And shall never again depart!

Joyously happy, she wanders along,
   Convinced she will view heaven soon;
Singing the while a strange wild song,
   To a weird unearthly tune.

Alone at the dead of a Winter's night,
   With no sign of the living near,
Her mind is filled with a full delight,
   And never one thought of fear.

Though the ghost-like trees shake their shivering
    boughs,
  And the Moon casts their shades o'er the way,
Though the winds wail weird, yet they cannot arouse
  A mind which is shrouded for aye.

At length she came where the roadway led
  O'er a river, whose waters wide,
Hurrying 'mong shadow and moonlight, spèd
  In a free unfrozen tide.

And from where she stood on the bridge above
  She could hear its silver song ;
For the wanton waves wove enchanting staves,
  As lightly they danced along.

And, listening intent, she stood gazing below,
  Where the river ran merrily by,
While her face was lit with a fervent glow,
  As of eager expectancy.

The moon was high, and the heavens were clear,
  And the fields were covered with snow ;
And no mortal sound struck on the straining ear,
  Save the song of the river's flow.

But Mary still looked on the glistening waves,
   With an ever-brightening glance ;
Still listened intent to the syren staves,
   In the dream of her terrible trance :

Till she started like one when a happy thought
   Has shot through the searching mind,
And ran down the bank to the fairy spot
   Where the rays on the river reclined.

By the margin she stood with her eyes enrapt
   By the brightness the moonbeams made ;
But she quailed as she glanced where the waters crept
   In the gloomy arches' shade.

But all fear soon fled, for her spell-bound eye
   Was fixed by that part of the stream
Where the ripples were 'llumined so beauteously
   By the Moon's ethereal beam.

Oh ! God of heaven, is there no one near ?
   Is there not one hand to save,
Ere this joy-lit face find a resting-place
   Beneath the ensnaring wave ?

"At last, oh, God, I have found," she cried,
  "The door of my heavenly home!"
And with one shrill scream, she sprang into the stream,
  And sank 'mid its snow-white foam.

The cry died away, and then all was o'er,
  And the river flowed calmly past;
And the crystal waves rippled as bright as before,
  Over one at rest at last.

Oh! the heavenly joy of a sorrow past!
  Oh! the balm for a broken heart!
Oh! the blissful rest which is gained at last,
  And shall never again depart!

.   .   .   .   .

All that unhappy day on which poor Mary,
Broken in heart and hopeless, left her home,
Jacob felt ill at ease at work, and thought
Only of her, trying to find some reason
For her sad manner, and, when coming home,
Resolved to question her, and share her sorrow
'Twas a dismal night, and glad in sooth was he

To view the village and his well-loved cottage.

Affecting all his wonted cheerfulness,

Lest Mary should be startled, in he went,

And found, as usual, everything in place,

And neat and tidy.   But his eyes, surprised,

Wandered at once unconsciously o'er all

For something missing, something that had ne'er

Before been wanting—Mary was not there !

At first he deemed her gone on some small errand,

And seated him to wait for her return.

The wind moaned loud, the shutters creaked and
        shuddered ;

And ever and anon the cloudy smoke

Came whirling down the chimney.   Round about

And over all there seemed to hang a dreadness,

Making the body shiver with an inward chill,

And silence brooding strained the listening ear.

All of a sudden thro' his anxious mind

Darted a fearful thought, unformed and vague,

And loud he called his daughter by her name.

No answer came.   .   .   .   The silence grew intense,

And made him frantic.   Forth into the night

He rushed unheeding, battling with the storm,

On through the village; and from shop to shop,
And house to house, ran like to one deranged,
Crying for Mary. But the astonished folks,
Ensconced by their firesides, could only stare,
And pity him. And from each cosy cottage
He braved the blast the deeper in despair.
At length, and after many a fruitless question,
He found a labourer who had passed his Mary,
When coming home from work. From him he knew
The road she'd taken, and, with difficulty
Procuring aid, set out in search of her.

For hours they fought against the wind and drifts,
And, searching every lane and ditch and hedge,
And wakening every house, that long night passed.

When the grey leaden light of early morning
Began to mingle with the waning moonbeams,
And over all the wakening world to cast
A dull, cold, lifeless hue, the wearied searchers
Found her they looked for. In a little bay,
Formed by a turning of the river's course,
Upon the wave-washed pebbles lay the body—
The weary, worn-out body of poor Mary.

E

Her flaxen hair was floating round her form
Like golden seaweed ; on her marble features
Beauty and sadness, peace and happiness
Rested together, with the same faint smile
That played upon them sleeping on the highway.
Her wearied soul had soared serene to heaven !
No words can tell the feelings that o'erwhelmed
Poor doting Jacob's half-bewildered mind
When he knew all.
                    The quiet little place
Was stirred as it had never been before,
And wrapt in sorrow at the dread event.

One lovely morning, when the bright cold sun
Shone clear above the peaceful snow-clad landscape
Mary was carried to the little churchyard,
And gently laid to rest beside her mother.
Many a tear was shed beside her grave,
And many a word of sorrowing solace said
To poor old Jacob, but in vain, in vain ! `
No balm but death can heal a broken heart !

The Spring had scarcely thawed the frost-bound earth
When Jacob, changed in form and feature, sickened :

He could not live without her, so he died.
And now the three lie sleeping side by side.

" And what," you ask, " befell the vile betrayer—
The ruin of a household?" Why, he lived
Just as before, giving himself no blame,
Perhaps not thinking any merited;
As many, many scoundrels like him daily do !

THE LAY OF THE LATEST MINSTREL.

CANTO I.

I.

Oh ! Muses nine (I think that that's the number),
   That dwell somewhere about Parnassus' hill—
A place where I should not incline to slumber,
   For fear of catching a rheumatic chill—
Pardon the faults which may my lines encumber,
   And let your courted inspiration fill
Each word and verse of this my lengthy lay,
And save it from a premature decay.

II.

But yet I cannot well be disappointed
   Though your refusal seals its dismal fate,
For the amount of verse lame and disjointed
   That hath been sent and forced on you of late,
Would wear the patience of a saint anointed,
   And put him in a far from courteous state.
It may, however, come beneath your glance :
If not, I must just leave its fate to chance.

III.

Now that I have invoked (like every bard
   Without a patron) all the Muses' aid,
The next thing is, of course, to have regard
   How all my powers can be best displayed—
A course which bards and Laureates aye discard
   When cash and Birthday Odes are to be made—
The first forsaking taste to win the Crowd,
The other pride to puff the puny Proud.

IV.

However weak or wandering be my strain,
   Let independence dwell in every note !
From affectation let my voice refrain,
   However harsh its melodies may float
Upon some ears ; nor let me slyly drain
The dews that gem some other's favoured flowers,
If on mine own coy Genius shed no showers.*

V.

Oh ! let me choose some half-unhackneyed theme,
   One not worn threadbare quite by such as I !
But where am I to find such ?   It would seem,
   On looking round, a hopeless task to try ;

There is one line awanting in this Stanza, but as it sufficiently expresses my
meaning, I did not think it worth while altering it.

For round each flower that yields a sweet there teem
   A billion bee-bards, barren all and dry,
Eager to get the honey anyway,
Stinging and stealing, striving as they may !

VI.

Avaunt ! oh, Plagiarism, and shut thy gate on
   Me for God's sake, for there are those within .
Thy guileful porch for ease that did thee wait on,
   Whom I do grieve e'er fell into such sin ;
For did not Tennyson prig from Michael Drayton
   The very song that did his war-fame win ?
And there are more by luring Fame disarmed,
Whom, passing by unguarded, thou hast charmed.

VII.

But I do sing nor for reward nor fame,
   Because I'm keen enough in sight to see
That now-a-days, though strong may be one's claim,
   'Tis oft ignored, oft never known to be ;
On Publishers I here put half the blame,
   And half on Critics' haste and bigotry.
So, save this style of verse which I am using,
I'll see that nothing's borrowed in my musing.

VIII

Oh ! fair Edina, my adopted town,

    Queen of ten hundred (more or less) church spires !

When of thy matchless beauty and renown

    Singing, even my poor modern muse ne'er tires.

Me it would ill befit to run thee down,

    Though thy funds' state some new town-tax requires ;

For thou art noble, though a bit in debt,

Like most of thine aristocratic set.

IX.

Where is the landscape lovelier than thine own ?

    Where is the hill more grand than Arthur's Seat ?

For lofty piles thou stand'st, indeed, alone,

    For men most learned, and for female feet,

Which (and to me the cause is quite unknown)

    . Are flat as flaps, and anything but neat ;

Thy Sons and Daughters—God repent that you

Should have to harbour such an icy crew !

X.

Thy *Sons* are all professional or sage,

    Brimful of bunkum, fashion, and conceit

(At least I give that as my humble gauge,

    Which please accept as you do think it meet) ;

Their names appear on Charity's *public* page,
   Yet are their desks with unpaid bills replete ;
They dress, and snub, and make it life's whole labour
To have high friends and be 'bove every neighbour.

XI.

Thy *Daughters*—well, as I have said above,
   Are beautiful, reserving certain parts,
But far too proud and Arctic for sweet Love
   To show himself in out beyond their hearts.
Thus Cupid hath but barely room to move,
   Far less good scope to throw his random darts ;
Whatever real their " shut up souls" contain,
Their present code of manners must restrain.

XII.

Oh ! place of Scotland's greatest, brightest, best !
   Haven of wit and wisdom in the past !
Seeing the stuff of which you're *now* possessed,
   God knows what will become of thee at last !
I doubt not you must scornfully detest
   The pigmies who have gradually amassed
About thy feet since that now distant time,
When breathed thy Giants, glorious and sublime !

XIII.

Thou hast thyself improved in *size*, I ween,
    But modern taste oft mars thy form, alack!
By placing things as they ought never been,
    All jumbled in a most promiscuous pack;
As will by minds unprejudiced be seen
    In such a group as Wilson, Scott, and Black.
If men *must* monuments to Provosts raise,
Let them be placed where Provosts win their bays!

XIV.

And *apropos* of monuments, I may
    Remark that those to Genius consecrate
Are not, alas! *all* worthy.   Just survey
    The thing the greatest of great Scotland's great
Hath reared to him, then turn in shame away,
    And sorrow that the town which sealed his fate
Hath not been kindlier to him.   But, however,
He's spared *one* sight that would have made him shiver.

XV.

Oh! fair Edina (as I've said before),
    Still, still of thee must be my strengthening strain!

Of thee and thine the more I sing, the more
   I long to launch forth into song again.
Yet though my effusions flow right from the core,
   I fear extremely they'll be all in vain,
For, having been 'mid petty pomp so long,
I hardly hope you'll like my simple song.

XVI.

And yet there's hope, for Poets now-a-days
   But seldom think of making you their theme,
Or such as you, but fill their laboured lays
   With twaddling subjects, such as they do deem
Are nearest to the style or tone which pays,
   Thus, wanton, wasting many a goodly ream.
If thou wouldst only patronise poor *me*,
I'd be most glad to write an Ode to thee.

XVII.

Thrice noble Town! (Now, that's a fairish start
   To this new stanza, which I wish to be
Faultless in form, in substance quite as smart
   As any that I've written previously;
That my deep sentiment I may impart
   In toto on a theme so loved by me)

Thrice no——, but no, I'll make it far more terse
(The phrase I mean), by heading a new verse.

XVIII.

Thrice noble Town !   Within thy precincts are
    Learning profound, and Beauty at her best ;
In church-going children thou excellest far
    The most of mothers whom I have addressed.
Thy godly women love a Church Bazaar,
    At which they buy or beg with Christian zest—
Although, I've heard, Bazaars are used as handles
To help the motion of the newest scandals.

XIX.

But this I do not credit, as to me
    They have an air of saintliness about them ;
For there no lotteries are allowed to be—
    The ladies think 'tis more correct without them.
The ministers, 'tis said, would like to see
    Them in again, though they are forced to scout them.
The reason, I am told, is that a raffle
Makes off with things which sellers' wits would baffle.

XX.

Thy people's cultivated taste is shown
   Once every week upon the Saturdays,
When they in carriages—now and then their own—
   Visit the Hall where Halle's Band displays,
Or where Miss H—— in some piece unknown,
   Lands the majority in a music-maze,
Which (Monday's *Scotsman* having been perused)
Is much admired, or critically abused.

XXI.

Now, do not think I mean to be abusing—
   For Romans must by Roman law abide—
Only I sometimes think it quite amusing
   How some are carried on by Fashion's tide.
If most of these but went by their own choosing,
   The Classic spate would very soon subside ;
But it is strange how prevalent is the passion
In drawing-rooms for music most in fashion.

XXII.

Yet don't mistake me, or pronounce me low
   In taste and training, or " a howling cad ;"

To " symphonies" and fugues I am no foe,
  But rather otherwise, yet I must add,
Enquiries into the *general* taste would show
  That it inclines just somewhat to be " bad ;"
I.e. it loves a song like " Scots wha hae,"
As well as any of the present day.

XXIII.

Of course, they show a praiseworthy docility
  In thus fulfilling th' exacting rules ·
Which sacrifice nigh all to save gentility—
  A thing that's taught in all our " proper" schools ;.
Though some do say 'tis far from true nobility,
  And that it makes its owners narrow fools.
But as *I* ne'er possessed one single tittle,
Of course my views must go for very little.

XXIV.

Edina ! Foster-mother of the Play !
  Long could'st thou boast a stage by all revered,.
The best trained, highest cultured of the day,
  And more than all by trembling players feared ;
For o'er it then true Critics wielded sway,
  And damned at once all worthless who appeared.

The times are changed, now everything depends
On that which London out of season sends.

XXV.

Of course thou yet hast actors of thine own—
 Thy histrionic fame is not dead quite
While J. B. Howard plays, as the Shaughraun,
 Three months per year, and on his benefit night;
For, while he leaves Shakesperian parts alone
 (Such as Othello) he gets on all right,
Or while his wife, as Rob Roy's spicy spouse,
Shrieks herself hoarse, amusing all the house.

XXVI.

But even with these thy glory's fast decaying,
 In this respect, from what it one time was;
To Begg's quotations and unceasing praying
 Against all things against Religion's laws,
A portion of the blame I would be laying;
 Yet that could scarcely be sufficient cause.
'Tis this—the profit's not from cultured classes
But off the things that satisfy the masses.

XXVII.

And so it is that now the good old plays—
 The works of writers which the world once moved—
The noble action that in Garrick's days
 A less advancèd generation loved,
Win but a meagre mite of scanty praise,
 While shallow stuff is by the crowd approved.
Alas ! that men of wit should stoop to write
Plays that but scarce survive the opening night !

XXVIII.

Why is the Drama thus allowed to fade,
 While men of genius everywhere abound ?
Has Literature become a common trade,
 Whose articles are sold so much a pound ?
Alas! our plays are all by contract made,
 Direct for them by whom the fee is found.
Drama is done, and in its place are writ
The low burlesque and witty worded skit.

XXIX.

Who will come forth from out the selfish throng,
 And write to save great England's honoured name ?

To such a noble one there shall belong,
   Not wealth perhaps, but lasting future fame.
His works shall live, while others perish long
   Before the grovelling minds from whence they came.
Ye who possess the valour to essay,
Arise, arrest the Drama's dire decay!

XXX.

Time-honoured Town, where Genius once did reign,
   In varied splendour, on a lofty throne;
Where gentle Ramsay wove his homely strain,
   Whom Walter Scott so proudly called "Mine own;"
And Burns, sore tempted, sadly wooed in vain—
   Why art thou now in letters nigh unknown?
Thy gifted sons are few and far between,
And ciphers to the mighty that have been.

XXXI.

Thy prose writers—behold a motley crew
   Of hard-up pulpit spouters, all intent
On making up a sort of decent screw,
   By sermons to the monthly papers sent;
Containing doubtful doctrines not a few,
   To which in Church they could not well give vent;

And scores upon the guineas who depend,
To whom, of course, the Muse may not descend.

XXXII.

Ah ! it is sad to look around and see
   A garden that was one time green and gay
Barren, but for the weeds that needs must be,
   And all its beauties blighted by decay ;
Or the once noble, winter-blasted tree,
   From which the winds have reft the leaves away.
Oh ! shades of Wilson, Scott, and Jeffrey, pity
The sorry state in which you've left your City.

XXXIII

Gone are the greatest Scotland e'er shall know !
   Her days of lettered glory long have past !
The tide that came in such a mighty flow
   Hath turned again, and now is ebbing fast ;
And threatens to become so very low,
   That we'll be left but slimy mud at last.
God grant some Light like Luna may appear
In this dark night, and draw the waters near !

F

XXXIV.

Of Poets there are plenty, it is true,
 At least of those who get that appellation—
Those who can write a pleasing verse or two,
 After long hours of steady application—
Though God alone is cognisant how few
 Deserve such dignity of designation.
Most men may rhyme ; but Thought and Sound, refined
By Inspiration, form the Poet's mind.

XXXV.

Of all contemporaries my humble song
 Will not attempt to tell, for I would fail
Even to enumerate such a mighty throng
 In any moderate space ; forby the tale,
Although told faultlessly, would prove too long
 For modern readers, and seem sadly stale.
I'll only mention here the more sublime,
And leave the others till another time.

XXXVI.

There dwelleth in this City one that's great
 In mental power, and learnèd—one by force
Of intellect who rose from low estate
 To be admired by all ; the welling source

Of whose pure verse is Nature.   Him had Fate
  Not favoured—Genius was his sole resource !
Hard was the fight ere all thou hast was won—
Self-cultured, gifted, noble Anderson !

XXXVII.

Long didst thou sing unheeded, long obscure
  And nameless 'midst thy daily honest toil,
Cheering the homely hearts of fellow poor,
  Yet laying stores of knowledge by the while ;
Until at length thy standing was secure,
  And high and low both praised thy sterling style.
Since then, thy wit hath eased the heavy woe,
And thy sweet pathos caused the tear to flow.

XXXVIII.

And then there's Smith, the ministerial Bard,
  Ambitious for a fame beyond his pews ;
Whom pastoral cares nor Session rows retard
  From paying his attentions to the Muse.
To him is justly due the rich reward
  Which he hath gained by publishing profuse ;
For Free Church folk are generally ascetic,
And very seldom rise to the poetic.

XXXIX.

His works are numerous, but throughout them all
    We plainly see 'tis a divine who writes ;
The sombre broad-cloth, like a darksome pall,
    Shadows each dainty morsel that invites,
And robs it of its light.   The Poet's call
    Is not unto the pulpit ; he indites
Lays of all things, brimful of melody,
And tuned to more than one particular key.

XL.

Not that by any means I would convey
    His musings make up one religious wail ;
For, promptly after each catastrophe,
    Or when a Bank's ambitious graspings fail,
He poureth forth the sympathetic lay
    In daily papers—and assists their sale.
" He's proved himself a Poet long ago,"
So says one Critic, and *he* ought to know.

XLI.

Oh, Blackie ! left to us of other days,
    When souls and minds like thine were not so few—

My pen the dictates of my heart obeys,
   In doing humble homage unto you—
Not only out of reverence for thy ' Lays;'
   But admiration of thee through and through ;
Vigorous in mind and body, wholly free
From taint of false conventionality !

XLII.

And there are signs of great things yet to be
   In the sweet verse from Robertson's young heart ;
Which floats as fresh as Spring winds o'er a lea,
   Uncurbed by Affectation's useless art,
That soils so much of our day's poetry,
   Yet gains its ready entrance to the mart.
If he but scorn contemporary fame,
His future efforts will embalm his name !

XLIII.

These, oh ! Edina, are thy sons of song—
   At least all those of any high pretension ;
Not taking into count the rhyming throng,
   Of whom at least some dozens I could mention.
Thy tastes, alas ! to *Art* do not belong,
   But all to argument and Church dissension.

Worse luck! your present foremost feelings' bent
Is not to verse, but Disestablishment !

XLIV.

But though it well might suit thy present state,
   I'll not give vent unto my humble views
Upon this matter, much discussed of late,
   And thereby risk the fortunes of my muse
On her first venture ; but will rather wait
   Till some critique my waning strength renews ;
And as, no doubt, I'll have to wait some time,
There'll be a chance of polishing up my rhyme.

XLV.

But everything must terminate, and so
   Edina, I must end this lengthy lay ;
For time and space are precious things, although
   I've plenty more that I would like to say.
And now, if thou, benignant, but bestow
   One gentle smile, it will me quite repay ;
And when of thee my work is worthy reckoned,.
I'll hurry up, and publish Canto Second.

TO INSPIRATION.

Hail Inspiration! coyest of dames,
Whose favours countless suitors seek in vain,
With lavished wealth, alluring to obtain!
'Tis not the hand profuse alone that claims
Thy cherished smiles.   For " many a time and oft,"
Passing the eager palace with disdain,
Dost thou refuse 'midst luxury to remain,
And, with shy Genius, in the wretched loft
Cheer'st the poor Poet's life, whose only pain
When thou art with him, is that he again
May sigh for thee departed !   Oh ! if thou
Would'st but reflect thy fire into my strain,
And lend me light, I'd struggle on amain
To win the wreath that decks the favoured brow.

THOUGHT.

Beloved Thought! Thou variegating flower,
Now pure and bright with Hope's ethereal hue,
Now dimmed with Disappointment's chilly dew—
Thou art my best companion! Many an hour
I've passed along with thee, soothing this life
With thy sweet perfume. Oh! had I the art
To plant thy wild seeds surely in my heart,
I'd reap a harvest of them rare and rife,
By studious cultivation! But the soil
Must first be rich and fruitful, and the streams
Of Learning's waters and the genial beams
Of Knowledge must, with much of care and toil,
Expand the germs, which, after all, but yield
Their rich autumnal fruits to grace a field
O'er which the sun is sinking.

G O D.

Almighty God! ˉJehovah! Endless space
And uncreate infinity are full of Thee,
Throughout the timeless ages of Eternity!
What power can limit Thee? What mind can trace,
Even in imagination's loftiest flight,
The confines of Thy presence? Infinite,
Eternal, and Supreme! Thou reign'st alone
In wondrous majesty, unseen, unknown,
Amid an awful mystery. Behold!
At Thine Almighty Word Creation rose
From the dark bowels of Chaos, to unfold
A token of the greatness that o'erflows
The endless Universe! Yet, even above
Thy mightiness, prevails Thy boundless love!

BEFORE THE BRIDGE.

Beside a fastly running stream I lay,
Watching the fleeting wavelets as they passed,
Now gleaming in the sun, and now o'ercast
By some tree's shade. Not very far away
It rose, a little spring, all bright and pure,
In rippling crystal, where white lilies grew
And breathed their sweetness, but, as on it drew,
The waters, widening, seemed to grow obscure
And noisier, until it reached the spot
Where I reclined, breaking o'er stony ground
With quick'ning pace ; then with a sudden bound
It plunged beneath the bridge. And then I thought
" How like to life ! The starting-place all bright,
The end enshadowed by Death's dreary night!"

BEYOND THE BRIDGE.

A sad, sad thought, and one I did not care
To harbour long ; so up I rose and went
Towards the bridge with pondering step, and bent
To trace the stream still further. Oh ! the sight
That met my eyes ! It thrilled me with delight
Ecstatic ; and the thoughts of dull despair
Were changed to those of Hope. 'Mong meadows sweet
With wildflowers' perfume, rippling melody,
Calmly it wimpled on towards a sea
Shining afar, that joined the arching sky
In blended loveliness. "This is," thought I,
" The type of life beyond the grave, replete
With rest and joyful peace." Let me not grudge
To sorrow here, to live " beyond the Bridge !"

THE PRIDE OF MAN.

Man's life on Earth is but one varied trouble,
Made up of vain aspirings, disappointments,
Joys that but whet the keen sharp edge of sorrow,
Fears which make dark the present, hopes which cheat
The future of its doubtfulness.   And all
Is of Man's making.   Pride, vain, hollow pride,
Worketh Man's misery.   Oh! that all but knew it!
Then would the light of Heaven enhance Earth's darkness,
For Earth would be the stepping-stone to Heaven.
But men seem blind to true advantages,
And weave their own misfortunes.   Why should one
Despise and trample on his neighbour, both
Being of one loving Father ?   Man's real bliss
Is found in yielding others happiness !

. MAN'S VANITY.

When one but contemplates Man's littleness,
How ludicrous seems all his self importance!
The Earth is wondrous in its magnitude
To Man, containing an infinitude
Of mysteries, far beyond his understanding ;
Yet of the planets Earth is of the smallest—
A grain of sand 'mong pebbles on the sea-shore ;
And the most mighty spheres we know revolve
Around the glorious centre of the Sun,
Which, in a mighty fellowship, will yield
Its homage to some vast unknown creation,
Beyond our pigmy powers to imagine ;
Yet feeble Man, strong in his own conceit,
Deems the wide Universe prostrate at his feet!

EARTHLY HAPPINESS.

One thing is graciously denied to Man:
The knowledge of the future.   Hope is half
The happiness of Life, time that has gone
Yielding the other half.   Griefs that have passed
Leave oftentimes the sweetness of a joy,
And pleasures that have left us long ago
We taste again, refined in recollection;
And the unmeasurable blank before us
We fill up with our fond imaginings,
Brightened and beautified by the touch of Hope.
Thus with the dim reflections of the past,
And the vague dreamings of a time to come,
We modify the sorrows of the present—
Poor Man, whose happiness is but a shadow!

THE THOUGHT OF DEATH.

Many there be who wend their way through life,
Engrossed supremely in the world's affairs,
And vainly purposing to make Life yield
Its own reward.   Nigh every selfish thought
Their minds possess, excepting only one—
The thought that every mortal hath to die.
This by some means they manage to evade
In its intensity.   Such men are as
The traveller, who in the darksome night
Heeds not the warning that a horrid chasm
Yawns in the roadway further on, and dashes
Reckless along, to meet his desperate fate.
'Tis well we should be mindful of our end :—
Death is but feared by those who on themselves depend!

D E A T H.

What can there be about the simple thought
That we must die, which causes us to shun
Its dreaded recognition more than aught
That haunts us here on earth?   Let everyone
But weigh the matter well, and there is naught
To fear within the tomb.   'Tis but the door,
Though dark and drear maybe, and grimly fraught,
That leads us from the world when life is o'er,
To never-ending peace.   When Jesus died,
And tenanted the tomb, He left the ray
Of Heaven's celestial light, and purified
The blackness of the grave.   So, let us pray
Tht: when the sombre portals do appear,
Through faith with welcome we may hold them dear,.
As guiding us to God !

TO A· BANK NOTE.

The Fates decree, and I must say farewell
To thee, my cherished one, whom I would fain
Within the precincts of my purse retain
A little longer.   Fancy dare not dwell
Upon the blank that thy departure makes
In my poor pocket, which, when thou art left,
Of everything like money is bereft.
And even Hope my fainting heart forsakes,
And vanishes with thee, for where to turn
To find another such " I am to learn."
Yet, after all, it really is a wonder
That thou hast been so long my constant mate
When all thy friends have fled.   Oh ! cruel fate,
That drives us two so very far asunder !

SPRING.

The reign of Winter's over now, for lo !
  The rills dance merrily down the steep hillsides,
  And through the plains the river swiftly glides,
With all remaining of the vanished snow.
Upon the trees the sprouts begin to shew ;
  The birds are busy, pluming the tattered wing
  And so can find but little time to sing ;
  The lark now mounts to meet th' uprising day,
  And dew-drops nestle where the hoar-frost lay—
For Spring's sweet breath is felt where'er we go.
  Here is a snowdrop, bending its fragile head,
  As if against a storm it seems to dread ;
  The primrose blooms in every mossy glen,
  And Nature, waking, robes herself again.

AFTER A SUMMER SHOWER.

The clouds are passing o'er the brightening plain,
And Sol, emerging, reassumes his reign;
The rain-drops glisten on each leaf and blade,
Purer than rarest jewels.　From the glade
Floats the rich music of the blackbird's song
Upon the odorous west wind.　All along
The dark green hedges chirping sparrows fly,
And the glad larks are caroling in the sky;
The summer shower has swoll'n each little rill
That rhythmically tinkles from the hill;
The woodlands ring that were erstwhile forlorn,
And the strong sunbeams raise the fallen corn;
In all its glory, varied and serene,
God's arch of promise spans the beauteous scene.

· AN AUTUMN NIGHT.

It is an Autumn night, and in the air
   There is a frosty keenness, for the year
   Is wearing old : the heaven's broad vault is clear
And cloudless, and the Moon reigns everywhere.
The trees are outlined dark against the blue ;
   Down in the hollow lies the peaceful lake,
   Slumbering in shade, save where the moonbeams break
   Silvery upon its bosom through the leaves ;
   And on the slopes the corn in golden sheaves
Is brightly spangled with the falling dew.
Oh ! what a scene of loveliness combined
   With peacefulness !   But as my way I tread,
The fallen leaves and chilly air remind
   How soon the Winter's snows will shroud fair Nature dead.

OCTOBER.

The Summer's gone : now Autumn wields her sway
   Over the fading scene.   The withering leaves
   Fall gently rustling ; and around the eaves
Each rose is blown, and blighted by decay,
And chill winds tear the petals fast away.
   The corn is cut : each field is bleak and bare,
   No notes of birds float through the misty air,
Save when the lapwings raise their piteous cry,
Or seagulls, fearful of the frowning sky,
Forsake the troubled ocean's heaving breast,
   And shriek along the plain.   Round every tree
   The restless east winds moan incessantly :
The heavens are clouded from the East to West,
And Sorrow's seal seems everywhere impressed.

IN WINTER.

The crisp white snow lies deep on moor and hill—
  A striking contrast to the dark thin trees,
  That shiver sadly in the biting breeze—
And all the melody of Nature's still;
For frozen fast is every mountain rill,
  And fled to shelter all the Summer's choir.
A lonely redbreast on the window-sill
  Seems envious of the genial kitchen fire,
Where snug we sit, after a day's work done,
Watching the setting of the cold red sun.
  Now to the East thick threatening clouds arise,
  Leaden of hue, and fill the bursting skies;
  And as I make the shuddering shutters tight,
I grieve to think where some may sleep to-night.

TO MY MOTHER AT CHRISTMAS, DURING
A PAINFUL ILLNESS.

Oh ! may this Christmas bring unto thy heart
   Joy for the present, hope for future days ;
And may the faith in Jesus' love impart
   The patient peace which every grief allays.

The year that's swiftly wearing to its close
   Has been to thee a time of weary pain ;
But as the mild Spring melts the Winter's snows,
   Bright, beauteous Health will comfort thee again.

The tear-dimmed eye that hath not closed in sleep
   Looks longingly to greet the lingering morn,
For in the heart, at every morning's peep,
   Dead aims revive, and sanguine hopes are born.

And when Aurora breaks the Eastern sky
   With rosy smiles, and Day brings up the rear
In glorious state, the Soul wings up on high,
   And for a time seems safe from every fear.

Thus is it now.   The New Year anyway
   Had brought, indeed, some happiness to you ;
But brighter now will be that festive day,
   For buds of health are flowering into view.

So, glad and thankful, hopeful for the best,
   Striving for strength and doing all we can,
We'll wait and trust, and God will do the rest,
   And thus the year will end happy as it began.

ODE TO MY SISTER.

I.

My darling Sister,

I long have purposed writing you in rhyme

My thoughts on you, and various other matter

Concerning things occurring daily that are

Of interest, but have never yet found time;

In fact, oft missed a

Goodly chance of doing something lasting,

I have no doubt,

Through being out,

When properly I ought to have been paying

My humble dues

Unto the Muse,

Whom no amount of prayers, or feasts, or fasting

Will ere move to

Give up to you

The precious favours lost by your delaying;

For you must know,

It is not always one can make to flow

The liquid line, and cause each word to glow

With force and fire,
But only when the centred mind
Feels a strange power undefined,
And an innate desire combined,
To tune the lyre.
But I shall try, now that I have begun,
To make amends
With pen and ink;
And now, I think,
The only thing to fear is when I'll stay
This little lay,
For certain pieces which I've lately done
Are without ends.

II

I do not know
Whether 'tis well or worse for me, my soul
Is nearly always under the control
Of love of things below—
Not sins, but things which wit or beauty show.
Thus, I adore
The company of her or him who gives
The mental food on which my pleasure lives,

And, even more,
Fair Nature's loveliness, lavished the whole world o'er.
But far above
These changeful likings rests the changeless love,
Which Earth's perfection could not one jot move
From its position
Within my heart—the love that prompts each feat,
And glows with light, and joy, and hope replete,
Even in my worst condition.
But, of course,
You easily anticipate its source :
It is for her than whom but God alone
Can claim a greater share of my affection,
And you and those who, 'neath her kind protection,
And by her weary toil, have nought but ease e'er known.

III.

Oh ! 'tis to her who now is stricken low
That all our joys, our very life we owe;
For did she not, when lonely with us left,
And unprovided for, of friends bereft,
Who in her affluence had friendship vowed—
Did she not then, when Poverty's black cloud
Hovered all horrid o'er our helpless heads,

With all its fearful train of wants and dreads,
Exert her fainting strength, by Love renewed,
And shield us from its bursting fierce and rude?
Yes, by her toil and care unceasing we
Have never known what misery may be!
Not only this : but, scorning to descend
In her proud spirit, and on friends depend,
With not one hand to help her save her own
And that of God, which never hath been known
Yet to forsake the pleading one, she strained
Her every nerve for love of us, and gained
Not only food and clothing, but a share
Of education such as would compare
With that of those whose aid, thank God, though offered,
Was aye refused as coldly as 'twas proffered

IV.

Ah! we can never fully recognise
The debt by us due to our darling mother.
It is a debt of love which can be paid
By love alone.   It is by gratitude,
Affection, and obedience that we ought
Show our appreciation, heart and soul felt;
Letting escape our lips no bitter word,

Or rude or wilful, watching every act,
And ruling our behaviour so that nought
May be therein to cause the slightest chord
Of grief or shame to vibrate in the heart,
World-tried and torn full many a time for us.
This is our *duty!*   Let love make it light,
And change it with his wondrous alchemy
Into a heavenly pleasure for our souls
To revel in delighted, and on Earth
A greater one we shall not wish possess.

v.

But let me end
A theme so high,
One which my weak Muse never would pretend
To satisfy;
And turn my lay
To sing the song intended while I may,
For, as is usual, I've a lot to say.
The first thing I'll discuss
Is pretty well beknown to both of us.
'Tis that which lies
Sometimes beneath a very thick disguise,
Sometimes quite bare,

In places where
Fair Nature pines for her diminished share
Of patronage.
It is the wedge
Placed 'neath the form of Beauty, with a view
Of perfecting the figure deemed askew,
And adding greater loveliness thereto ;
Which always must deface
Where there is perfect grace.
'Tis that—but no,
Why should I further with description go ?
Here's the summation—
The bitter bane of breathing here below
Is Affectation.

VI.

How sad to see
So many fools beneath its slavery,
Taking such painful heed
Of every word and deed,
Lest Nature fair
Shew unaware,
And, truthful, lay the whole deception bare.

Some of these seek its false enticing aid
To make them what they never could be made
                By any art,
                And play a part
In which even what they have is left all undisplayed.
                Some, from vain pride,
Wishing to rank in all things side by side
                With those far higher,
Don Affectation's thin disguise to hide
                All they require.
                While others, deep of mind,
Or beautiful, perhaps, but yet inclined
                To love attention,
By picking words, and studying all their acts
Oft mar the very lustre which attracts.
                And I could mention
Full many another species of this blight
                In man—*all* ages ;
But only it would take too long to write
                So many pages !

                VII.

                It is to me
(Because so rare) a joyous sight to see

A man, and more a woman, wholly free
From this foul taint;
For at the present Fashion seems to be
Nature's restraint!
And even though
The person, true to feeling, be below,
Or high above,
I would for her or him contract, I know,
A sort of love—
At least a combination
Of that and admiration.
And this is why,
For now of years a goodly number, I
Have tightly kept my hold of that stout tie
Of Love which holds
Within its folds
Our allied hearts, all eager and unalteredly.
For it is wound
All round and round
Each smallest corner of my heart, and bound,
Full sure and sound,
By bonds of admiration and attraction
Of that sound sense and honesty of action
So seldom found.

VIII.

Here let me say,

I trust that you, by any things I've said

As to my doctrines, will not be misled

In any way;

For next to Affectation, false and vain,

Vulgarity in girls I most disdain.

However pretty,

Or sharp, or witty

The girl may be,

If Rudeness be where Modesty should dwell,

Her forward talk and manner but repel,

And Love's incipient feelings quickly quell—

At least with me.

A gentle grace

Oft wins more lovers than a pretty face.

And this is rightly so,

For Beauty's brightest glow

Lasts but few days, even in its loftiest place—

While worth and sweetness stay,

To ease the weary road,

And guide us to the Way

That leads at last to God !

IX.

There is a class

Of giddy girls for whom I do not care,

But who, alas !

Are anything but rare.

This kind of girl

Loves constantly to live amid the whirl

Of some excitement—frivoling in the dance,

Or acting heroine in some sham romance

Of her own scheming ;

And such like idle dreaming.

Her shallow mind

Delights to count the numbers who pretend

For her a love, of very doubtful end,

And, pettedly, to favour or offend

When she's inclined ;

But, you will find,

That such an one is oftenest left to wend

All in the lurch,

Alone to church,

Through the cold years which single she must spend.

This, you will see,

Is meet to be

The only termination of the life

Of such a chit,

Which ne'er could fit

The woman for a good and faithful wife.

X.

Full many a life

Has been embittered by one haughty glance,

That might have been spent happily perchance,

And robbed of all the blessings that enhance

The endless strife.

Oh! melancholy surely is the lot of him

Whose dreary days are darkened by the whim

Of one false woman! How his hopeless heart

Must ache and bleed beneath the wilful smart!

His nights go sleepless and his days dawn dark,

And on his brow pale Sorrow sets her mark;

Life seems a useless series of pains,

And not one undimmed hope of Heaven or Earth remains.

This could not be

The state of things with anyone like me;

For, I am sure,

My love could never possibly endure

Without return.

But yet there is a love, like smouldering coke,

Which, damped, sheds round itself a clammy smoke,
Yet its strong flames the waters fail to choke—
Which deep down burn.
Oh ! then beware
Of cutting words, or cold or scornful air,
Lest aught be in thine answer
To breed the horrid cancer
That eats into the soul, and sheds gloom everywhere !

XI.

Next let me say,
One weighty fault of ladies of to-day
Is want of depth of mind,
With wit and grace combined.
Thus when we find,
Once in a way, a woman of high thought,
And in the Arts and Sciences well taught,
She generally lacks that tenderness
Without which Woman must be all amiss,
However clever ;
And hardly ever
Have I found one not more or less like this.
And, on the other hand,
The most of modern maidens seem to've planned,

When in men's company,

To talk but foolery,

Deeming, no doubt, that it's most in demand ·

Now, though most healthy men

Like nonsense now and then

When they get nothing more,

Even from them they adore,

It soon proves tiresome and becomes a bore.

How this should be

I hardly see.

Is it too far

To stretch one's fancy safely, to assume

That in the far-off future there shall bloom ·

A race of girls, without or gaud or gloom

To spoil or mar

Fair Beauty's grace, or Learning's lightened face?

XII.

But of this scrawl you must ere this have tired,

And if that's so, I'm near the end desired.

Try every way,

With ardent love and gratitude, to pay

The debt that's due

To one who never grudged to work for you.

Still let thy heart
Contemn the trammellings of useless art,
And let the flow
Of honest feelings from the soul ne'er know
Undue restraint,
Like to those hypocrites who, before they shew
The world their feelings, make them undergo
A careful paint.
And yet be free
In word and action from vulgarity,
Letting thine accents fall soft and refined,
Bearing the burden of a balanced mind;
Careful of scandal let thine utterings be,
Yet all untouched by sly hypocrisy;
Let Patience keep thy temper in its place,
And teach thy heart to yield with seemly grace;
Let a clear Conscience keep thy mind serene,
And watchful Virtue guard thy name from spleen;
Let Resignation soothe thy soul in grief,
And in good time will come the wished relief;
But chiefly, see thy breast be free from sin,
And fit for thy dear Saviour dwelling in;
Live good and godly, so that you may die
In perfect peace, and live again eternally!

ODE TO MY DEAR FRIEND, H. M. M. R.,

On His Birthday.

The Muses on Parnassus' hill
Could scarce into my mind instil
Enough to form a worthy lay
To greet thee on thy natal day.
For how with words could I impart
The speechless throbbings of my heart?
Had inspiration been my dower,
Had I possessed the Poet's power,
The sweetest lilt, the loftiest strain,
Had been alike but vile and vain
To ease my soul, and thus convey
The endless things I fain would say

If, curious, one should ask me why
The strength of song I thus deny;
The answer brief and bold would be—
" 'Twould take well-nigh Eternity
To tell, e'en in the swiftest line,
And twice Eternity in mine,

The blessings, wishes, hopes, and fears
My heart hath for his future years."

Then, as the bitter Fates decide
Oblivion must my wishes hide,
Since of the power my mind is scanted,
Just take what I'd have said for granted.

But though expression may not be
To those dear thoughts I have for thee,
Yet "Memory's aid" I do not lack,
So, with her leave, I'll hie me back
To sweeter scenes of other days,
And wander 'midst the golden haze
Which spreads around, and makes them seem
The joy-lit phantoms of a dream ;
And find the spot where we two met,
And trace the path we're treading yet :
So that the way we've yet to wend
May be lit up by Hope serene ;
For why should future days, my friend,
Not be as bright as those we've seen ?

Where *did* we meet?   The wearied sun
Had sunk upon the horizon,

And peaceful Evening's gentle light
Was ushering in a Summer's night:
'Twas that sweet time when labours cease,
And softening shades engender peace
Within the soul, and harmony
Dwells all around, that you and I
First made that friendship, which nor spite
Nor envy hath been fit to blight,
Though both have tried with all their subtle might !
When Memory, sullen, doth refuse
To grant the charm that life renews,
And I no more may see us stand
When first we grasped the mutual hand,
Deep may oblivion shroud my head
Amid the chaos of the dead !

My home was far, and there was none
Sufficient of my heart had won
For me to love, as Friend to own,
And I was really all alone—
Alone with Hope, alone with Fear,
With every joy, and every tear—
Until I found more than I sought,
When us two Fate together brought.

To thee my boyish heart was bared
With thee my inmost secret shared.
Scarce did my mind one thought contain
But what thou shared'st its joy or pain.
This was the 'channel where the woe
Of my young heart found room to flow,
When many a time the pent-up grief
Had overflowed without relief.

Day after day our friendship grew,
Day after day it proved more true,
Chequered full oft by tiff and huff
Which made the roadway rather rough.
But though I ofttimes lagged awhile,
You waited at the next road-stile
Till I came up, and having met,
We journeyed e'en the closer yet.
For when apart we always prized
The tie the more, and recognised
The folly of a hasty temper
Keeping two friends thus separate *semper*.
Oh ! bitter, bitter was the strain
Of jarring thoughts, and sharp the pain
Of deep remorse whene'er the cloud

Of friendship parted was allowed
To gather round, and all our pleasures shroud!

When love first caused my boyish heart
With all its fancied pains to smart,
When but one theme my lips would own,
And oped to speak one name alone,
How tiresome it must all have been,
And yet no want of patience seen
In thee, but, listening to the end,
You proved a sympathetic friend.

Then when my schoolboy errors drew
Down on my wayward head their due,
Or for some other had my name
Blackened to all in public shame;
When boon companions shrank from me,
As one bleached with vile leprosy—
While the disgrace should have attached
To those who would in sins have matched
Satan himself, oft have I seen
Thine advocacy intervene
To plead my cause, and thus defend
A grateful, though an erring friend.

How oft, when Summer's scented breath
Scarce stirred the leaves in Tyrell's Heath,
And softly through the sultry air
The birds made mellow music there,
When, 'midst the grass of richest green,
Blue violets were scarcely seen,
As sweet they hid their matchless eyes,
Like bashful maidens, when the skies
Hung cloudless, arched, and Nature smiled
In sunbeams on her beauteous child—
How oft have we together strayed,
And viewed th' enchanting scene displayed !
There we have told our stories o'er
Of other friends, and days before
We came together; there advised
Each other's doubts, and plans devised,
Which, not possessing what we willed,
Were very seldom e'er fulfilled.
Oh! how I long to roam again
The woods through which we wandered then:
In fancy only can I trace
Each beauteous walk, each favourite place,
Which seem, on looking back, to me
Some blissful paradise to be.

Oh! days that were, oh! distant days!
'Tis when with tear-dimmed eyes I gaze
Upon ye, now receding fast,
I feel my happiest days are past!

As I once said, some time ago,
My dear old friend, I do not know
What drew us two together so.
Our natures in most things are quite
As different as the day from night;
And many a squabble sharp and keen,
And heated argument I've seen
Betwixt us, yet there seems to be
A magnet placed 'tween you and me,
Which must at first have made us meet,
And guideth now our hasty feet;
So that, however much we try,
We cannot sever—you and I.

But why all this?   You know full well,
And better far than I could tell,
How things transpired.   Suffice to say,
Our love on this auspicious day
Still lasts, and stronger e'en than when

I dwelt with thee.   But here my pen
Grows soft and scratchy, warning me
I weary with prolixity ;
So, to the gentle hint attending,
I'll bring this missive to an ending.
With only this—May peace, content, and health
Be thine, till called upon to lay them by ;
And may you gain by Life the noblest wealth—
In Heaven and Mind an immortality !

ODE TO MY FRIEND, J. M.,

On the occasion of his Birthday, 14th May 1881.

I.

Dear M———,
'Twould be unfair if I were to let go
This day without remitting you some token
        To prove to you
        That friendship true
Which, since its birth, has never once been broken
        By word or act,
        Tho' oft, in fact,
By heated converse very much exposed.
        And, therefore, I hasten
        To legibly place in
The records of History, so far's in my power,
        The date of your birth,
        And your wisdom and worth,
By the few verses afterwards disclosed;
        Which, you will see,
        Are meant to be
Nor elegant nor classic, but a shower

Of lines promiscuous, and of words that rhyme,
In no set time,
Which, to prevent mistaking, you must know,
Is an address
To thee, J—— M——.

II.

What can I say
In feeble words t' immortalise this day,
The future reddest-lettered of the month of **May**—
Time's best division?
Shall I, in glowing terms and faultless verse,
Your every merit and your worth rehearse,
Without the least excision?
No! for the Muse's wings are far too slight
And inexperienced to attempt an height
Beyond her vision.
All she can do (and that she does with zest)
Is to acquaint all those as yet unblest
In ignorance of the fact,
That thou wert born—
Most probably in the very early morn—
'Mong hopes and fears,
And your own infant tears,

Just one and twenty years
Ago exact.
That fact alone, more than all I could say,
Must surely mark its memory to endure alway.

III.

Springtime has gone,
And not a few of Summer's suns have shone
Over the ripening scene.
The snowdrop has drooped in the southern air,
And the freshness has gone in the gaudy glare
Of a sultry Summer's sun.
The little green shoots of the corn have grown
Into waving stalks, and the buds have blown,
And mantled the woods in green.
The heather smells sweet on the purple hill,
And the birds with sweet music the woodlands fill,
Singing till Day is done.
Thus the Springtime of life with you now is past,
And the Summer is come, but, ah! not to last;
For Autumn, so solemn and sere,
With its withering leaves, will be here,
Chilling the zephyr's warm breath,
Then into the past it will also melt,

I

And the piercing cold frosts will be keenly felt,
Changing all life into death.
For, twenty-one years you have acted your part
Upon the rough boards of life's stage. . . .
But, however, believe me, it is from the heart,
I rejoice in your coming of age.

IV.

Twenty-one !
A fortunate day in the lives of the few,
When the wealthy heir
Claims his coveted share;
But nothing to me or to you !
Bringing us neither gift nor gold,
Nor right to great estate;
But showing us that we are growing old,
With nothing to cheer or elate.
And as this is so we must harder strive,
If we want to rise to fame;
And with plenty of pluck we may yet contrive
To leave—well, some kind of a name.
Twenty-one !
What a distance it seemed not so long ago,
When childhood's eyes looked o'er the way,

And gazed thro' the vista of years all aglow

    With hopes to be reached ere that day!

Yet how soon was it gained, and our hopes unattained,

    Though shining before us the same;

For the colour of distant hopes always remained,

    Tho' it glided away as we came.

        Twenty-one!

A turning-point in many or for good or ill,

A trying time, when all the passions fill

      The harassed mind,

      And every kind

      Of wanton wiles

      And tempting guiles

Are laid, and lead astray, oft even against the will,

      Then take thou heed

      Of word and deed,

Working with zeal, and having hope in front,

Yet putting not excessive trusting on't.

    For, that our future may be bright,

    We must work *now* with all our might.

And as thou hast been (greatly to thy praise),

Still be opposed to all of wicked ways.

V.

'Tis only when one leaves the family circle,
And all the friends of youth, for some place distant,
And strange companions, that their real value
Is rightly known.   Ah! what a gracious boon
A mother's presence is!   Oh! how it soothes
The grievèd soul, and cools the harassed mind
With loving tenderness!   How it reproves
Our wayward acts, tho' ne'er an angry word
Fall from the gentle lips!   It is an element
In Nature to restrain, to guide, and bless,
And teach us to adore the God who gives
Such guardian angels to us here on earth.
Here, dwelling lonely, distant from that spot,
Where are the ones far dearest to our hearts,
How often do the thoughts, spontaneously,
Dwell on them all, and in our mental body
Are we among the group!   How carefully
We should conduct ourselves and rule our actions,
When that same dear one whom we love to think of
Is constantly beside us in our thoughts,
And trustful, only sees us do correctly!

VI.

For you I see,
Forth in the future but prosperity,
If in the years that lie
'Tween this and then you constantly apply
Yourself to train yourself, even as you've done
In years through which you have already run.
For obviously,
Your tastes are after business naturally.
And with determination,
And steady occupation,
When ratiocinations
Have dispelled hallucinations,
And all your solid senses
Are free from all offences
Of arbitrary prejudice,
Neuralgias and biliousness,
Eccentric views and notions,
Which cause so many commotions,
Whenever they come in contact
With anything that proves a fact—
You doubtlessly will rise above the common crowd,
And cause the one who calls thee " friend " be proud.

VII.

How many an aim

We cherish now with hope to future fame,

Or ultimate success ;

Not thinking of all those who did the same,

And ended in distress !

For somehow, we can hardly preconceive

That all the dreams in which we now believe

Will fade away ;

For now we judge of dangers by those which we've passed,

And, eager, deem the next as easy as the last

To our essay.

But soon we know,

After a little, that this is not so,

And early find

Obstacles numberless before our footsteps laid,

Which to elude, at the dire toil dismayed,

So many men had from the right path strayed,

And fallen behind.

And then we understand

How hard it is to do what we have planned.

For tho' we try

To clear some ditch with all our utmost force,

We often land halfway, and then, of course,

We take some time to dry!

Thus even altho'

We strive and strain,

With might and main,

And never quail,

We often fail

To make the point proposed, and stop a good way down
below!

VIII.

And in what, my friend,

Will all our plans and future struggles end,

And when?

Only in death, and when our bodies blend

With the same earth on which we now contend,

And not till then.

For tho' we gain,

By weary work and long, a goodly store,

It only stimulates us to attain

The more.

And so

The term of life allowed us here below

Must needs be fraught with much of every woe;

All consequent

On discontent,

And a desire

To rise still higher

Than what we are,

And rest some place, which ever keeps afar

But do not think

That I would have you from your labours turn,

Or plans repent.

No! work as you will, but only try to learn

To be content,

Then you will get thro' life with ease, and happy be

With your reward, and, looking back, will see

A life well spent!

IX.

Ah me, alas!

How quickly do the years of boyhood pass,

Leaving us men,

And a good way off from that tranquil bay

Where the waters were sparkling and bright as we lay,

Moored safe by parental care!

For soon did Ambition come and steer

Our frail eager barks from the coast so clear,

Out to life's stormy sea,

Where now, even when

We've a sort of foreknowledge of what is before,
How the waves will surge, and the winds will roar
    In fearsome hostility,
We ever keep on through the battling waves,
On, ever on, till we find our graves,
    And sink in Eternity !
    But is this, then, all—
All that we gain by the voyage of Life ?
Is there no reward for the hopeful strife,
    At length to sweeten the gall ?
Oh, yes ! there is one, but 'tis far, far away,
    Far through the waves and the wind ;
And not to be reached till we've toiled o'er the sea,
Guided by Faith, that by Grace we may be
    Worthy the rest we shall find !

LINES ON POETRY,

WRITTEN FOR A LADY IN AN ALBUM.

My dear C——, 'tis, you know,
Impossible to cause to flow,
In crystal waves and mighty force,
A streamlet, muddy from its source.

True **Poetry** is like the bow
That in the heavens its form doth show,
When showers of rain have over past,
And sunbeams through the clouds are cast.
It cometh not with frost or snow,
Nor when the bitter East winds blow;
But when sweet April—vernal Queen—
With varied mood enchants the scene,
In perfect form, and purest hue,
It compasseth the glistening view;
It strikes the eye as nought can do,
And sets the mind a-wondering too,
That such foresights of Heaven should be
Vouchsafed to beings such as we.

Yes, Poetry is nigh divine—
The loftiest of the lofty Nine
Who on Parnassus' hill preside,
And loveliest, gentlest, best beside !

When Genius' light burns bright and clear,
The clogs of Fancy disappear ;
From showers of doubtful thoughts revolved,
A glorious form is fast evolved.

To speak in line that's fit to scan
Is possible to every man,
And even woman ; but to sing
With powerful depth or clear sweet ring
Of God and Man, is only given
To those great minds inspired from heaven.

Some seek to find (who never can)
The hidden, wondrous talisman,
That changes barren human words
To sound like harmonising chords.
If *it* lie not within the breast,
Then, though we seek from east to west,
The magic power will be as far
As souls in Hell from Heaven are.

Some may by perseverance gain
The art to form a pleasing strain,
Like this, perhaps, but there they stay,
And things they write with them decay.
But there are words will never die,
Lips that shall speak eternally,
Minds that will ever foster mind,
Men to be loved by all mankind!
Immortal fame, immortal praise,
Are theirs who sing immortal lays!
Such is the meed of but the few—
Those who received the work to do,
And did it well; those who, with pen
And brain, toiled on for fellow-men:
Who sang, without a false control,
The deep, true feelings of the soul—
Lending the World a light to see
The secrets of humanity!

Poetry is the purest wave
Wherein the soul of man may lave
To soothe his sorrow, and allay
The pain inflicted on the way
Through worldly life.

He loses life
Who giveth to the earthly strife
His heart and soul, and never knows
The joy of rest, save Death's repose.
Oh! soar above the common end
Of man, and thus prove man's best friend!
If every mind had love of gold
And friends alone, how cold, how cold
The world would wax.　Pale struggling Thought
Would die, or soon be brought to naught,
Till Mind, disgusted at the sight,
Would leave the Earth in sorry plight.

But, thanks to God! there yet are found
Men of great sense and love profound,
Who lift us up, and let us see
Things far beyond the common range that be.

A SUMMER RAMBLE.

Listen how the birds are singing,
And the echoing woodlands ringing!
Hark, the music of the stream,
Dancing in the sun's bright beam,
Kissing wild flowers as it passes,
Peeping pretty through the grasses,
Growing on each emerald side
Of its golden crystal tide!
Look, o'er every meadow gay,
Where the tender lambkins play,
Golden cups and daisies white,
Beauteously their charms unite,
And through all the humming air
Send a perfume fresh and rare!
Through the shady woods and valleys,
Glittering plains or high-hedged alleys
As my wondering way I take,
Little birds their music make,
As they chirp on every tree
In a faultless harmony.

O'er the welkin, bathed in blue,
Not a rain-cloud meets my view,
But from Morning's natal place,
To where Sol hides his glowing face,
Noontide's golden rays are sending
Brightness with all beauties blending.

See in yonder verdant meadow,
Underneath that tall tree's shadow,
Oxen languidly reposing—
Sometimes chewing, sometimes dozing;
While around their blinking eyes
Countless myriads of flies
Float, and of their blood partaking,
Keep the drowsy loungers waking.

Here's a farmer bent on knowing
How his youthful crops are growing,
Walking with each horny hand
Stuck athwart his breeches' band.
Inwardly he's making notes
Of his barley, wheat, or oats—
Whether this is strong or slight,
Pure or blackened by the blight:

Or, as his eyes all anxious gaze
Where his sheep and cattle graze,
Trusting they may only thrive,
That for once he may contrive,
With all his store, in any way
To make the game of farming pay.
But, however much his need,
I doubt if he will e'er succeed.

As my all-enraptured eyes
View this earthly Paradise,
And my thirsting, listening ear
Drinks unsated all I hear,
Sinks my mind in mild repose,
And my soul with joy o'erflows.

Evening shades have now begun
To mar the splendour of the sun,
As with slow and stately march
He traverses the western arch;
While the brightness of his rays
Is softened by a golden haze
Spreading, like a fairy gauze,
O'er his face as he withdraws.

Here, down by the river side,
Near the gently flowing tide
Breaking silvery where I stand,
On the pebbly glittering sand,
From my feet to where the sun
Rests upon the horizon,
One bright path of gold extends,
Gleaming, glancing, till it ends,
And with heaven's own glory blends!

In the East the coming night,
Softly stealing o'er the sky,
Lends another, calmer sight,
In a shady harmony.
Where the river meets the sea,
Darkening clouds are rising fast,
And their shadows gradually
O'er the rosy heavens are cast.
Pine woods growing on the side,
Lean their dark boughs o'er the river,
While the dying zephyrs glide
'Mong the foliage all a-quiver:
As the waters further flow
On towards the spreading sea,

K

Fainter still the outlines shew,
Till they're shrouded totally.

Over all the prospect wide,
Heaven or Earth, or east or west,
Harmony and Peace preside,
And a sense of coming rest!

A RHAPSODY.

Oh! let me away to yon brook to-day,
  And there recline,
Where the air smells sweet near the new-mown hay,
And the waters are clear as they dance away,
Singing the while with the birds a lay
   All divine;
   And the Summer sky,
   In a harmony
  Of golden haze and Italian blue,
  Hangs cloudless o'er the enchanting view,
   Changing ever,
  And reflecting a lovely and varied hue
    Unto the river,
    Rippling bright
    In the joyous light
    Of the sun above;
While the woods on the hill with a rapture ring,
And the zephyr shakes peace fróm its languid wing,
And the voice of the Universe seems to sing
    Only of love!
    There shall I gaze

On the numberless beauties the landscape displays
  With enraptured eye,
And longingly list to the love-laden lays
  That float me by.
   And my soul shall lave
   In the crystal wave
Of a pleasure which none may partake of save
   The unfettered mind,
   Which has left behind
The baser thoughts which fair Fancy bind.
   And there I'll stay
Till the gathering shades of the dying day
   Begin to creep,
And the glowing sun, wending his western way,
   Sinks into the deep.
   Then I'll hie me back
   To this world, alack !
   And perhaps will weep,
That the Fates should forbid such a joy should be lasting,
And that sin, lust, and greed should for ever be blasting
   All purity here ;
   Where, instead of a clear
Crystal fountain of happiness wherefrom to drink,
There's a foul stagnant pool into which we all sink,

'Twould appear.
Oh! when will the soul
Wield its blessed control
 O'er the mind,
In place of the lust
Which makes but vile dust
 Of mankind?

TO SUMMER LATE IN COMING.

Are these the signs of thee, oh! summertime,
   I see and feel now through the lengthening day?
   Or dost thou still thy flowery feet delay
In some far distant or more favoured clime?

Fain would I find thy presence everywhere,
   And feel thee breathing in the western gale;
   Yet while I search, the east wind's dismal wail
May spread again the bleakness of despair.

But o'er this landscape which mine eyes survey,
   Beauty and universal brightness dwell,
   And to my sanguine soul delighted tell
That thou art still true to thy first love, May.

And, hark! oh, joy!   I hear the cuckoo's call,
   Which in the Spring just passed we sought in vain,
   Sounding in monotone along the plain,
And mellowing the music murmuring over all.

The nightingale trills forth his melody
    Just as the lingering shades of evening fall;
    And in the woods the feathered songsters all
Chorus to him in blithesome harmony.

And far above, unseen, the skylarks sing,
    Lost in a beauteous maze of blue and gold;
    While at my feet, around me there unfold
Beauties on beauties, past my numbering.

Over the fields that darksome-like had been,
    While yet the seeds were only newly sown,
    The little shoots to larger stalks have grown,
Covering the ground with waves of tender green.

The grass, luxuriant in its emerald shade,
    Spotted with wildflowers, various in their hue,
    Serves as a beauteous foreground to the view,
And lends a freshness to each hill and glade.

The yellow primrose on the mossy ground,
    Born in the shade, and of a modest mien,
    And violets, clustering in the grass half seen,
Sprinkled with dew, in myriads abound.

And all the buds have blown upon the trees,
    And wild-roses and golden-blossomed broom
    Bedeck the roadside, whilst the sweet perfume
Of snowy hawthorn loads the languid breeze.

Hark! how the atmospheric music swells!
    Filling the soul with heavenly delight!
    While o'er each scene that glides upon the sight
Beauty, reposing in her glory, dwells!

Yes! Summer, thou art here! And joys attend
    Thy welcome advent to this longing earth;
    For every heart tastes of thy joyous mirth,
And earth with heaven seems for a time to blend!

HARMONY.

When the twilight's shades are falling
　　Over rosy Summer skies,
And the glowing Sun is shining,
On the horizon reclining,
　　Ere he dies:
How I love to wake the spirit
　　Of my organ as I play
Seated pensively alone,
By my window open thrown
In a calm and holy tone,
　　Some old lay!

For the music and the shadows
　　Blend in perfect harmony,
Which, through soul and spirit stealing,
Changes every mortal feeling
　　Utterly;
And the happy soul, o'erflowing
　　With a joyous ecstasy,
Seems on melody to soar
Unto Heaven's serener shore,
Where, restrained by Earth no more,
　　It is free!

LINES.

What will this life avail if Death doth end
The mind's existence? What if Man's true aim
Be to procure six feet of burial ground
For his tired bones to rot in? Then great Man—
Toiling, suffering, miserable Man—
Fares far worse than the lowest thing that crawls.
Mind yields to him a nobler, keener joy;
But ah! 'tis dearly paid for. Mental wounds
Heal scarcely with the potent balm of Time,
And leave deep tender scars. The human mind
Is the reflection of a heavenly light:
It is not *life*, but Life's ennoblement:
Mortality but curbs its liberty,
And limits its great range to worldliness.
But when the links that bind it are undone
By kindly Death—dreaded and much abused—
The cage shall crumble into vilest dust,
Mind like the joyous lark, a captive freed,
Will heavenwards soar, and mount eternally!

Then, if Man's value lie but in his mind,
And life be given but for mind's troubled birth
And cultivation, why should we endure
The utmost hardship and severest pains,
To be enriched with things that pass away,
And leave us barren at the latter end.
Wise men and fools, young hearts and well-experienced,
All seem to have one end—the gathering up
Of wealth! Oh! what a sorry sight to see
A man, born in the midst of rustic bliss,
Who, from the days of earliest boyhood,
Urged by the restlessness of proud ambition,
Hath toiled through many weary days to gain
What he can ne'er enjoy, struck grey by age
And verging on the grave! How vain, how vain
Hath all the struggle been! A lifetime spent
Seeking the rainbow's base! A fight well fought,
But only finished when the hands relax
In death, and cannot grasp the longed-for prize.
The brutes seek not the glories of the world,
Though wholly earthly. Yet we mightier beings—
The God-like owners of immortal souls—
Pollute and prematurely slay our bodies,
And mix our spirits with the foulest dirt,

And squander life to win some worldly wealth.

Oh ! vanity, which Death at last dispels,

When wilt thou flee from Man's deluded mind ?

God save us ! What can wealth or rank avail

When the wide grave is yawning for us ? Then

How hollow Earth seems ! Kings are but mere pigmies

Contrasted with the darksome mightiness

Of Death. The sighed-for, sinned-for name

Serves but to deck a headstone somewhat larger

Than a poor neighbour's. Pride and Poverty

Fall, and are buried on one battlefield !

Life is misspent if, when the end is nigh,

We cannot welcome Death. We could not taste

The sweetness of a joy not having sipped

The gall of sorrow. Death at first sight looks drear

And cold and pitiless, but, near at hand,

To those who face him trustingly, there lies

A tender look of deep benevolence

Half hid beneath his eyebrows, for he knoweth

From what an empty, profitless existence

To what a pure and perfect state he guides us.

The first touch of his hand is chill and clammy,

But soon the river's ferried, and the shore

On which he lands us reached. The more we strive

To turn our faces from him, and evade
His call, the more appalling he becomes.
His hour is fixed, he will not wait for us, –
However much we wail and beg on him.
And, as he surely at the time prescribed,
Will come to call us from our earthly homes,
. Most doubtlessly we should contrive to meet him,
Not as a foe, but as the friend he is.

This we can never do if in the world
We live but for the world.   Our thoughts must soar
Above the things around us, and consider
How we can get a little heavenwards.
Wealth is no gain, but goodness is a jewel,
Which, found on Earth, will light the way to Heaven !

ECONOMY OF TIME.

Swiftly the years pass o'er our heedless heads,
With all their opportunities and hopes and dreads,
Leaving us oft times void, unmarked, and profitless.

Till we, with fear struck at their rapid flight,
All suddenly behold the dismal plight
Our acts delayed and parts unplayed have placed us in.

Then at dear Life and Fate all-wise we rail,
Raising our voice despairing in the wail
Of dire distress, misfortune unavoidable.

On Earth our days are of but brief duration,
But while they last we have an occupation
High in its aim and end, by God assigned to us.

Therefore, take heed lest Time roll useless by,
That Life may lend you peace in which to die,
And a reward in Heaven be thine eternally.

REALITY.

When the soul is bowed down by the load of affliction,
Which wraps it in darkness and wearies it sore ;
When the crushed heart's despair breeds the dreary
    conviction
That Hope's faintest glimmer has gone evermore :

When the world is repulsive, in all its bright beauty,
When Nature's smile sickens, and Art seems in vain,
And the tired mind compels us, forgetful of duty,
To long for the grave's sure release from our pain :

When Fear crawls behind, and deep gloom reigns
    around us,
When even our purpose in Life is delayed,
When dismal forebodings and grim doubts confound us,
And urge us to ask why this world was made :

Oh ! 'tis then, only then, that we know the real value,
Of lemons, or rhubarb, or camomile pills ;
For the usual thing wrong, I may just as well tell you,
Is bile in the stomach—the worst of all ills !

VAIN LOVE.

I.

The evening sky
Hung in a harmony of hazy blue,
With golden streams of sunshine shooting through,
Far in the West, where sinks the tired Day-king,
When we along the lanes went wandering—
My Flo' and I.

II.

" Oh Love," I said,
" Nature is sweet around us.   Hill and vale
Are wrapt in peace, save for the nightingale
Trilling his song of love, all troublous stirs
Are hushed—save in my soul," and then on hers
My hand I laid.

III.

" Stupid !" cried she,
And into quite a flood of laughter broke,
That all the echoes of the woodlands woke,

And scared the brooding silence of the scene;
Then frisked away, light as a fairy queen,
        From me, ah me!

IV.

        Moan winds, oh moan!
For the rich harvest of my hopes entombed;
Moan for the bright buds blasted ere they bloomed;
Sing to my soul sweet strains of soothing woe,
And let the theme be but my darling Flo'—
        Lost, yet mine own!

TO THE SPIRIT OF POETRY.

I loved thee, fairest of the Nine,
  And deemed my love returned,
When listening to thy strains divine
  My soul enraptured burned.

I thought to worship at thy shrine,
  And make an offering meet ;
To bask beneath thy smile benign,
  Contented at thy feet :

To linger near and fondly hear
  The music of thy lyre,
As soft it floats in measured notes,
  And taste its heavenly fire.

But though my heart with longing smart,
  And all my soul is thine,
My sole return is that you spurn
  My unpoetic line !

TO MARY DISTANT.

Could thy mind know the feelings that flow through
　　my heart,
　As I look on Life's beauties all dimmed by despair;
Could'st thou know what it is to be banished apart
　From the object adored, and yet still to love there :

Could my weak words but barely pourtray the condition
　That Love unrequited envelopes me in—
Your kind ear would list to my humble petition,
　And either my Heaven or my Hell would begin !

TO MARY.

Dear Mary, to thank you with words for the token
　That tells me your kind heart is mindful of me,
I needs must employ all the best ever spoken,
　And that, I am sure, would prove tiresome to thee.

My heart overflows, but my language has left me,
　My brain teems with fancies no tongue could express;
Of my poor power of speech my deep joy has bereft me,
　And thus 'mid my pleasure I'm plunged in distress.

The lily is lovely; each modest flower hiding
　Beneath its pure petals its sweet bashful eyes,
Like a gentle young maid in the world confiding,
　Ere long she has seen through its hollow disguise.

I shall gaze on it oft, I shall keep it beside me,
　It may be a little, it may be for years;
And shall think on the giver whatever betide me,
　But *one* day, ah! me, I shall view it through tears!

TO MARY.

When thy words of love are spoken,
    I'll be chary;
'Tis by such that hearts are broken,
    Oh, my Mary!
Sweet the potion Love distils,
How it soothes and how it thrills!
Seeming balm for all the ills
    We endure!
But, when portioned out by sips,
Tempting just the longing lips,
    Then it kills.
For the fierce and wasting fire
Of unsatisfied desire,
    Deep and pure,
Breaking soon thro' all control,
Devastates the harassed soul,
And Death's clammy grey mists roll.

TO KATIE.

Maiden with those laughing eyes,
　　Welling o'er with girlish glee,
Did'st thou ever recognise
　　What a charm thy form could be?

Did'st thou ever in thy play
　　Deem that thou could'st conquer one
Skilled in love, and wield a sway
　　O'er this heart as thou hast done?

No! ah, no, thy mind serene,
　　Knows nought else but love of fun,
Though thou reign'st a very queen,
　　Served and loved by every one.

The rose might woo the butterfly,
　　Or the grass the fleeting dew,
With as much of hope as I
　　Tell the love I have for you!

T.O E. L.

.Enchanting Lady !   Mistress of thine art !
Fain would I bring an offering unto thee
From one enamoured of the gentleness,
Inspiring love insensibly within
Each heart that hears the music of thy voice.

Lovely in form, in feature all refined,
Instinct with grace and modesty combined ;
Sweet is thy manner, but far sweeter still
The trembling accents, cadenced at thy will.
Oh Lady ! worthless each poor halting line,
No human strains can sing of things divine !

TO ISOBELLE.

I.

Isobelle, Isobelle,
What can thy charms excel?
Who can withstand the spell
    Cast by thy beauty?
Surpassingly pretty,
Sarcastic and witty,
Looking so lovely, to love and adore thee
    Seems but my duty.

II.

Isobelle, Isobelle,
Nought can my love dispel,
Nothing but Death can quell
    Love's wild emotion!
Wilt thou not hear my plea?
Wilt thou not pity me?
Give but a hope to me, and I shall strive to be
    Worth thy devotion!

TO THE SAME.

I.

My hope has gone, my joy is o'er,
'Twas but a dream, and nothing more;
A sweet delusion of the mind,
Which round my heart its folds entwined,
And held it captive, tightly bound
With chains and bars of love profound.
But now 'tis past—Farewell, farewell,
My only hope, my Isobelle!

II.

Why did we meet if but to part?
Why did I love to break my heart?
Why did I ever soar so high?
Why did I live, if but to die?
For hope was life, and hope has fled,
And I but live as I were dead;
For evermore farewell, farewell,
My loved, my lost, my Isobelle!

TO THE OLD LOVE !

Though the words were cruel and cold
That my dismal fate foretold,
In the blank of years unrolled,
  Yet I wonder
If thy one love-glowing heart
Feels in memory one smart
For the ties *Death* was to part,
  Rent asunder ;
If thine eyes, so blue and bright,
Lit once with Love's lambent light
Ever through the lonely night
  Shed one tear
For the exile from thy sight,
  Once so dear. ·
For you loved me once, you said,
  And I know,
True love never can grow dead,
  Here below ;
For if real it abides
In the heart, whate'er betides,
E'en although its object chides,

Wounding sore.
Thus, if you spoke faithfully,
Thoughts must sometimes sadden thee,
Sighing for a time, ah, me!
Now no more!
Do not, then, increase my pain,
Hard to bear,
By affecting to disdain
Him who did thy love obtain,
When thou of his grief, 'tis plain,
Hast a share!

AN EXPLANATION.

I.

I left you, dear, because I knew
   Your love was growing cold ;
I saw you tried to bear me true,
   But could not as of old—
Another face had won the heart,
   So fond of me before ;
My words and smiles could now impart
   Their wonted charm no more.

II.

My soul was sick and sad, and yet
   I hoped from day to day
Your love, re-lightened by regret,
   Would chase the change away ;
But from your lips the fire had fled,
   The welcome from your eye ;
The rootless rose had withered dead,
   And so I said Good-bye !

MY STAR.

The night was calm, and the sky was clear,
  As I sat by my window thinking
On her whom my inmost heart held dear,
  And watching the stars a-twinkling.

And as I gazed on the heavenly scene,
  A little star caught my eye,
Shining so sweetly, and all alone,
  And I loved it—I know not why.

Dreaming of her, and of love returned,
  I centred my thoughts on that star;
For it shed a new brightness o'er my mind,
  And sent me a hope from afar.

But alas! as I gazed on its loveliness,
  It fell from its heavenly height,
And broke the sweet spell that had held my heart,
  And left me alone with the night.

The spell was broken, the dream was o'er,
  And the sky became overcast;

And the waters of sorrow o'erwhelmed my soul,
 And I wept for the hope that was past.

Ah! the sign was too true, for my love hath gone
 With my hopes to her home on high;
And empty and sad will life seem to me,
 Till I meet her again by and by!

THE LOVER.

AFTER KIRKE-WHITE.

The hour is late, and from the distant skies
The twinkling stars shed forth their quivering light ;
And weird the lonesome night wind softly sighs,
Breathing a sadness through the still midnight.

Here by my casement at this dreary hour,
When other eyes are closed in peaceful sleep,
I watch, regardless of Sleep's potent power,
And, wakeful, Love's devoted vigils keep.

Oh ! can it be that my poor longing heart,
Still led by Hope, eludes the consciousness
Of early death—which bids such dreams depart—
And sanguine sees afar some future bliss ?

Ah, no ! those pitying stars will sadly shine
Over the place where I shall shortly lie ;
And when at rest no longer I repine,
The winds regretful o'er my grave shall sigh !

VAIN REGRETS.

'Tis over now.   The anxious hours are past,
The hours of thoughts conflicting, fears unformed,
And hopes unrealised—hopes that made sweet
Life's bitterness, and brightened up my way.
And yet not once I recognised the light
Till reft away.   Ah, me! the day is dark
And night is dismal when the soul is sad!
My love, my love, oh! thou wert dear to me!
And yet I knew it not.   When thou wert still
Within my call I heeded not, but deemed
The vanished joy would last.   But while I dreamt,
And wavered in my purposes, alas!
All suddenly another stole away
Thy presence from me, and the paradise
That I had dwelt in so unconsciously
Was changed—so sadly changed!   All happiness
Was gone, and in one awful moment
Dissolved the beauteous bowers of blissful thought,
Leaving the landscape barren.   Oh! my love, . ,
Gone, gone for evermore!   Why did my heart
Not earlier know itself?   Then had these tears

Ne'er burned my aching eyes.   Indeed, I dreamt
The while thou wert so nigh me, and I knew not
Thou wert so much to me ; or 'twas perhaps
Thy presence in itself that gave to me
Sufficient bliss, and kept my thoughts serene
From dwelling on the future.   Oh ! but thou,
My lost for ever, wert the only one
My mind and soul had cherished constantly !
Through all the changes of a varied life
Thy face was present to me.   When amidst
The 'witching glances of far haughtier maids
The memory of thy constant tenderness
Made others dwindle in comparison
With thee, my darling.   Now, ah ! now, farewell,
Farewell for ever, for it must be so.
My hopeful fears sink in fell certainty,
My fearful hopes are tumbled in the dust,
The happiness of hopes and fears is dead,
And life seems useless, for my love is wed !

THE NEWSBOY.

I.

Fastly and thickly and coldly,
The snowflakes came hurrying down,
　　In an eddying crowd,
　　And spreading a shroud
Of pureness and peace o'er the town.

II.

Empty and dreary and lonely,
Every street, alley, and square,
　　For the wind, I ween,
　　Was cold and keen,
And the snow was deep everywhere.

III.

Barefoot and ragged and wretched
Shivering and blue with the cold,
　　Crouched a poor little form
　　From the heedless storm,
With a bundle of papers unsold.

IV.

Weary and drooping and hungry,
Hoarse with the unheeded cry
   A home he has none
   Till he's sold every one,
And so he must onwards and try.

V.

So, hopeless and homeless and heart-sore
Still he went wandering on,
   With the same sad cry,
   And no one to buy,
Till the last flow of strength had gone.

VI.

Then weary, so weary, and dying,
He laid his poor head down to rest
   On the cruel hard stone,
   But ere morning shone
He had lain on his Saviour's breast.

VII.

Rigid and lifeless, but peaceful,
Cold in a doorway he lay
But his face was bright
In the morning light,
For its sorrow had vanished away!

SONG.

TWILIGHT FANCIES.

When the folded flowers are sprinkled
  With a Summer evening's dew,
And the stealing shadows softly
  Veil the fastly fading view:

When the Sun hath died in glory,
  Far beyond the purple hill,
And sweet melodies are tinkled
  By each rippling mountain rill:

When a harmony surrounds us,
  And our minds are wrapt in rest,
It is then with painful pleasure
  Love-thoughts throb within the breast.

But when Morning breaketh brightly,
  All the dreaming dies away,
And the fancies of the Twilight
  Vanish in the busy day!

THE MILLER'S SONG.

I.

Oh! the wealthy man may look with scorn
   On the lot of a man like me,
And the Proud may pity the lowly born
   And deem it a charity;
But I heed not the sneer of the puffed-up Peer,
   Nor the pity of Pride desire,
For my heart is light, though my fortune's slight,
   And what more can a *man* require?

Chorus—

   While the wheel goes round,
   And the corn is ground,
  And the sparkling stream flows by,
   No care need I share,
   And no frown shall I wear,
For there's no one so happy as I,
    As I,
  There's no one so happy as I!

II.

When the harvest field is full and fair,
   The merrier life to me ;
And when Fortune is fickle I do not despair,
   But trust she may kindlier be.
And I think it too bad to say life be sad,
   While it yields us a joy or a friend ;
For if conscience be clear we shall ne'er want good
     cheer,
   And a bright hope on which to depend !

    While the wheel goes round, &c.

"THE AULD HOOSE."

The auld hoose stuid by a burnie's side,
That wimpled sae bonnie an' bricht,
As we weanies wid wide in its glistenin' tide,
Frae the lang summer morn till nicht;
Aye runnin' aboot, noo in an' noo oot,
Happy as birds, an' as free,
We scampered an' played 'neath the auld hoose's shade,
For 'twas a' the big warld tae me.

    The dear auld hoose, the queer auld hoose,
       Whatever my fortunes be,
      Wi' its gabled en', an' its but an' ben,
       It'll aye be dear tae me!

And there in the e'en I hae aften seen,
Aifter their wark wis done,
My faither and mither a' sittin' thegither,
Watchin' their wee bit son.
An' oh ! I can mind a' the glances kind,
An' the anxious looks they'd gie,
As I sported sae crouse roun' the dear auld hoose—
Far the happiest hame tae me.

      The dear auld hoose, &c.

It's thae looks sae kind that will ever bind
My thoughts tae thae days o' yore,
For I love to gaze, e'en through memory's haze,
On the faces that are no more.
For as mony's I meet on the daily street,
There's nane half sae welcome tae me,
An' when memory strays to thae bygone days,
It's the lang-lost smiles tae see.

  The dear auld hoose, &c.

An' as I look back on the cosy thack,
An' the cheery wee bittie o' grun',
Whaur ma niither wad sit wi' her wark an' knit,
An' join in my innocent fun—
I dicht my weet face, an' picture the place
A' lonely an' thick wi' decay,
An' wearily sigh for the boon but to lie
Near the auld hoose fading away.

  The dear auld hoose, the queer auld hoose
   Whatever my fortunes be,
  Wi' its gabled en', an' its but an' ben,
   It'll aye be dear tae me.

WILLIE AND I.

I.

'Twas Springtime, and Nature had newly arisen
From her slumbers within Winter's bleak frosty prison,
The snowdrop and primrose were decking the vale,
And the odours of budding flowers perfumed the gale;
We were children, and life was but newly begun,
And we knew nothing else save our innocent fun,
When my Willie and I roamed the hillside together,
And sported in glee 'mong the fresh mountain heather.

II.

The shadows were falling, an' evening serene
Had followed the heat of a bright Summer's day,
And the gloamin's calm peace brooded over the scene,
And chased every thought of the world away;
We were wand'ring together whilst, warbling above,
The blackbird was trilling in amorous tone,
When my Willie confessed to his pure lasting love,
And I knew that the true heart I loved was my own.

III.

The ripe corn was waving beneath a hot sun,
And the work of the harvest-time newly begun,
And the rich scent of roses was borne on the breeze,
As it languidly moved through the leaf-laden trees,
The year was matured, and all Nature was bright,
And every heart throbbed with a joyous delight,
When Willie and I were made one by Love's tether,
And our loving hearts bonded still closer together.

IV.

The snows of the Winter are lying deep now,
Every leaf has forsaken each bare blackened bough,
And the wind whistles shrill as it sweep o'er the lea,
And sighs a sad dirge round each dead withered tree;
But although we are old, and our hair is as white
As the snows that are falling so thickly to-night,
We are happy as ever, and only await
For the Sun that will shine on our heavenly state!

GOD, FROM A WORLD, &c.

God, from a world of weariness
    I lift my saddened cry;
Oh! shew me how to seek Thy peace,
    And teach my heart to try!

Let the soft lustre of the light
    Of Thine almighty Word
Chase from my soul the clouds of night,
    And lead me to my Lord.

Teach me to know that Jesus died
    Upon the accursed tree
To save my soul, and crucified
    The sin that holdeth me.

Thus, guided o'er the doubtful way,
    And safe through darkness past,
The morn of Heaven's eternal day
    Will dawn for me at last!

" GOD SHALL WIPE AWAY THE TEARS FROM THEIR EYES."

Whate'er we do, where'er we go
     In search of peace of mind,
To make us happy here below,
     We only sorrow find.

For every hope, and every love
     Whose centre is not God,
At length must fail, and, shattered, prove
     Additions to our load.

Thus is our fleeting worldly life
     A dreary winter night
Of stumbling faith, and grievous strife
     To gain a little light.

But night will yield unto the day
     That waits us up on high;
And God at last will wipe away
     The tears from every eye!

"BEHOLD I STAND AT THE DOOR AND KNOCK."

Far had I wandered from the fold,
　　Where Jesus' flock are fed,
And thoughtless strayed at will where'er
　　My lust for pleasure led.

But all throughout that dreary night,
　　And 'midst th' exciting din
Of worldly ways, I thought I heard
　　A pleading voice within.

And, taken with the gentle tones,
　　I listened, and I heard,
" Oh! wilt thou longer shut thy heart
　　Upon a loving Lord?"

Then bowed in shame I oped the door,
　　And cried, " Oh, Lord, forgive !"
And Jesu straightway entered in,
　　And now my soul shall live !

JESUS, TAKE MY SOUL TO THEE.

Saviour, unto Thee I call,
 From a world of misery ;
Free me from its guilt and gall—
 Jesus, take my soul to Thee !

Black and bleak the dreary way,
 Far as mortal eyes may see ;
Guide me, then, or I shall stray—
 Jesus, take my soul to Thee !

Oh ! the burden of my sin !
 How it wears and wearies me !
Oh, that I were pure within—
 Jesus, take my soul to Thee !

Look upon my failings, Lord,
 Not in wrath but graciously ;
Make my will with Thine accord—
 Jesus, take my soul to Thee !

Wash me in Thy precious blood,
    Spilt on Earth at Calvary ;
In that soul-reviving flood—
    Jesus, take my soul to Thee !

Weary, weary is the road,
    Girt by sin and death's dark sea ;
Oh ! relieve me from my load—
    Jesus, take my soul to Thee !

Lord, how long can all this last ?
    When at length shall I be free ?
Oh, that Life and Death were past—
    Jesus, take my soul to Thee !

[Rest, impatient soul, oh, rest !
    Sinful even thy longings be ;
At that hour Thy Lord deems best,
    He will surely ransom Thee !]